For Lindy

THE STRANGE TALE

OF THE

BLACK AND WHITE GOD

By

JEFF SHANKLEY

Printed by Flyer Press Ltd

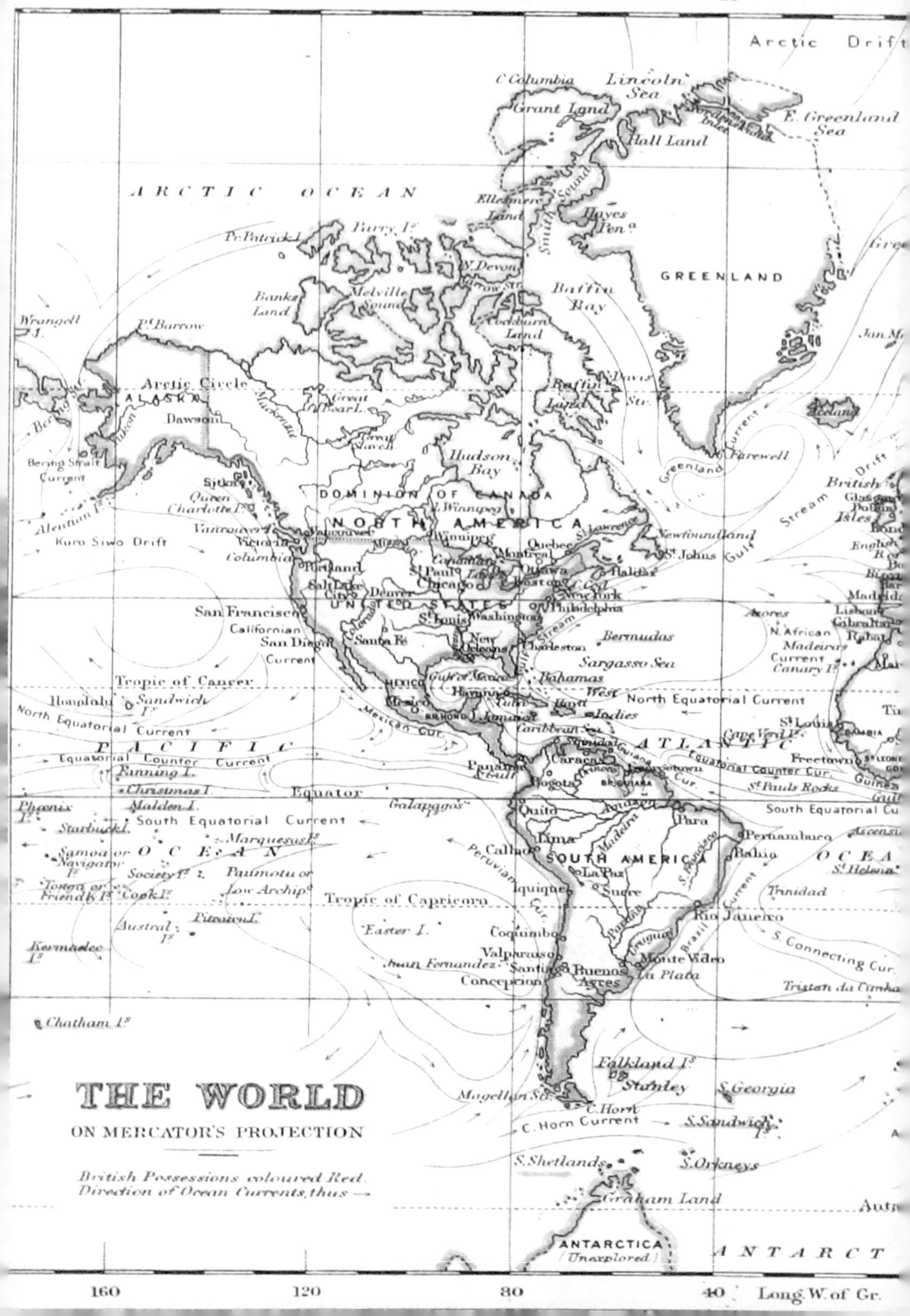
THE WORLD
ON MERCATOR'S PROJECTION
British Possessions coloured Red.
Direction of Ocean Currents, thus →
160
120
80
40
Long. W. of Gr.
ARCTIC OCEAN
Arctic Drift
C. Columbia
Lincoln Sea
Grant Land
Hall Land
E. Greenland Sea
Ellesmere Land
Smith Sound
Hayes Pen.a
Parry Is.
Pr. Patrick I.
N. Devon
Banks Land
Melville Sound
Baffin Bay
GREENLAND
Cockburn Land
Wrangell I.
Pt. Barrow
Jan Mayen
Arctic Circle
ALASKA
Yukon
Dawson
Mackenzie
Great Bear L.
Baffin Land
Davis Str.
Iceland
Great Slave L.
Hudson Bay
Greenland Current
Farewell
Bering Strait Current
Bering
Sitka
Queen Charlotte Is.
DOMINION OF CANADA
L. Winnipeg
British Isles
Aleutian Is.
NORTH AMERICA
Vancouver I.
Victoria
Vancouver
Winnipeg
Quebec
St. Lawrence
Newfoundland
St. Johns
Gulf Stream
Kuro Siwo Drift
Columbia
Portland
Montreal
Ottawa
Halifax
Salt Lake City
Denver
St. Paul
Chicago
Boston
C. Cod
New York
Philadelphia
UNITED STATES
San Francisco
St. Louis
Washington
Azores
Lisbon
Gibraltar
Madrid
Californian Current
Colorado
Santa Fe
New Orleans
Charleston
Bermudas
N. African Current
Madeiras
Canary Is.
San Diego
Sargasso Sea
Bahamas
Tropic of Cancer
MEXICO
Gulf of Mexico
Havana
Cuba
West Indies
North Equatorial Current
Honolulu
Sandwich Is.
Mexico
BR. HOND.
Jamaica
Haiti
Mexican Cur.
Caribbean Sea
Cape Verd Is.
St. Louis
North Equatorial Current
PACIFIC
Trinidad
Caracas
Guiana Cur.
ATLANTIC
Equatorial Counter Current
Panama
Bogota
BR. GUIANA
Freetown
Equatorial Counter Cur.
Fanning I.
Christmas I.
St. Pauls Rocks
Equator
Galapagos
Quito
Amazon
Phoenix Is.
Malden I.
South Equatorial Current
Para
South Equatorial Cu
Starbuck I.
Marquesas Is.
Pernambuco
Samoa or Navigator Is.
OCEAN
Callao
Lima
Madeira
SOUTH AMERICA
Bahia
Peruvian Cur.
La Paz
Society Is.
Paumotu or Low Archip.
St. Helena
Tonga or Friendly Is.
Cook Is.
Iquique
Sucre
Trinidad
Tropic of Capricorn
Brazil Current
Pitcairn I.
Austral Is.
Easter I.
Parana
Rio Janeiro
Coquimbo
Uruguay
S. Connecting Cur.
Kermadec Is.
Valparaiso
Monte Video
Juan Fernandez
Santiago
Buenos Ayres
La Plata
Concepcion
Tristan da Cunha
Chatham Is.
Falkland Is.
Stanley
S. Georgia
Magellan Str.
C. Horn
C. Horn Current
S. Sandwich Is.
S. Shetlands
S. Orkneys
Graham Land
ANTARCTICA
(Unexplored)
ANTARCT

40
80
120
160
Franz Josef Land
Spitzbergen
ARCTIC OCEAN
C. Chelyuskin
Anjou Is.
New Siberia
Liakhov Is.
Taimyr Pen.a
Barents Sea
Bear I.
Nowa Zemlia
Kara Sea
North C.
Arctic Circle
White
Archangel
SIBERIA
Lena
Yakutsk
Obi
Yenisei
St. Petersburg
RUSSIA
RUSSIAN EMPIRE
Stockholm
Riga
Moscow
Kazan
Perm
Tobolsk
Tomsk
Omsk
Irkutsk
L. Baikal
Sea of Okhotsk
Nikolaevsk
Petropavlovsk
Sakhalin
Kurile Is.
Amur
Angara
Irtish
Nijni Novgorod
Orenburg
Saratoff
Volga
Danzig
Berlin
EUROPE
Vienna
Kiev
Odessa
Buda Pesth
Rome
Black S.
Astrakhan
Caspian
Aral Sea
L. Balkash
ASIA
Gobi or Shamo
Vladivostok
Mukden
Khiva
Samarkand
Constantinople
Smyrna
Aleppo
Teheran
Bokhara
Yarkand
Kabul
Peking
Sea of Japan
Japan Is.
Tokio
Yokohama
Black Stream
Kuro Siwo or
Damascus
Ispahan
CHINESE EMPIRE
Hoang Ho
Tripoli
Alexandria
Cyprus
Suez
Cairo
Kelat
Lhasa
Nanking
Shanghai
Basra
Persian Gulf
Karachi
Delhi
Benares
Yang-tse-kiang
PACIFIC
Tropic of Cancer
Medina
Mecca
INDIA
Calcutta
Mandalay
Canton
Formosa
Hong Kong
Suakin
Bombay
BURMA
Hainan
Mariana or Ladrone Is.
N. Equatorial Cur.
Khartum
Aden
Arabian Sea
Hyderabad
B. of Bengal
Rangun
Bangkok
Manilla
Philippine Is.
L. Chad
Socotra
Madras
China Sea
Saigon
OCEAN
AFRICA
Berbera
Monsoon Cur.
Ceylon
Colombo
Penang
Labuan
Malacca
Caroline Is.
Gilbert Is.
Maldive Is.
Singapore
Borneo
Equator
Mombasa
Equatorial Counter Cur.
Sumatra
Bismarck
Zanzibar
Seychelles
Chagos Arch.
Batavia
Ellice Is.
Leopoldv.
Amirante Is.
Sunda St.
Java
Solomon Is.
Rotumah I.
Massumba
INDIAN
OCEANIA
Equatorial Current
Zambezi
Mozambique
Madagascar
Fiji Is.
BRIT. S. AFR. CO.
Bulawayo
Mauritius
Mozambique Cur.
Reunion
Tropic of Capricorn
New Caledonia
West Australian Cur.
AUSTRALIA
Brisbane
E. Australian Cur.
OCEAN
Perth
Norfolk I.
CAPE COLONY
Durban
Sydney
Port Elizabeth
Adelaide
Retrograde Current
Agulhas
Melbourne
Auckland
South Australian Cur.
S. Paul
New Amsterdam
Bass St.
Tasman Sea
Tasmania
Hobart
Christchurch
NEW ZEALAND
Marion I.
Crozets
Dunedin
Kerguelen
OCEAN
Antipodes I.
Heard I.
Auckland I.
Macquarie I.
Drift Current
Circle
OCEAN
ANTARCTICA
(Unexplored)
Long E. of Gr.
40
80
120
160

LIST OF ILLUSTRATIONS

ACKNOWLEDGMENTS

Deep gratitude to my son, LLoyd, for answering my endless questions.

Special thanks must be given to Lisa and Clyde Whiley for their endless support and encouragement.

Holly Gallant and Jonathan Trotter of FlyerPress for their patience and guidance.

Lindy Houseley for reading it a thousand times.

And last but certainly not least my dear sister Betty for a lifetime of support and for giving me the paradise of Sri Lanka to write in.

EPIGRAPH

The blue grasses in the spiritual mountains of Maharashtra, stir.

The heat! The heat! Relentless heat!

Tired murmurs are carried on the wind and anxious clouds begin to gather like nervous flocks above the broiling earth, cracked and tinder dry.
Whispers of the monsoon strike madness in the blood and Kali rides the wind fanning the flames,

leading man and beast to frenzy.

PROLOGUE

Isandlwana

There was a silence in the smoke that drifted through the shadows of men. The smell of blood and flesh decaying.

The vanquished and the dead.

The broken spears pierced the scorching bodies as they writhed in agony, crawling through the smouldering earth.

Voiceless,

bereft of sense and pain he waited to be carried from the bleeding hills of carnage in a limbo between life and death, between Heaven and Hell.

But no-one came.

Buried beneath the mutilated body of his dying horse, its stomach steaming and bleeding into the mud, he caught the creature's eye.

One last look.

One silent goodbye, as the light dimmed.

Only a gentle drifting now. An empty disembodied flight above the wandering ghosts, above the treetops, above the clouds as black as pitch, now white as snow.

Above the silent parade of terror and the carnival of slaughter.

Beyond the haunting whispers, beyond the futile sacrifice of elusive glory and the mocking grin of war etched upon the faces of each mother's son.

And there.

Through the smoke of man's anger, a leopard appeared, noble and dignified, and carried him upon his back, laying him down upon a bed of white feathers, each lighter than the heart.

And Ingwe covered him with Illshlangu sprinkled with muti and Iklwa to seek the lost spirits.

'Rest Baba, Shadow of Shaka, rest now with the swallows.

And begin the journey to yourself.'

1.MAHARASHTRA. WESTERN GHATS. 1882.

Six months later.

'Rākṣasācā vadha karā! Rākṣasācā vadha karā!'

As soon as night had fallen the villagers swarmed into the mountains, thirty or forty screaming in anger.

Burning torches filled the air with black smoke and the sharpened spikes of wooden spears drove the creature further into the darkness. His gruesome face turned and was lit in the glare of flames thrust towards him, before he scrambled further into the cave.

The screams of violence echoed as they cornered him and plunged their bhala one by one into the black body covered in blood and crying in agony. The frenzy continued until the deformed body lay motionless.

'Rākṣasācā vadha karā! Rākṣasācā vadha karā!!'

The villagers stood in silence, and then began to laugh hysterically. A laughter bred of fear. And then falling silent, they stood around the body, prodding it, watching rivers of blood pour down the rivulets of the cave.

The body stirred and slowly rose, the leather flap which covered his face fell away and its horrifying deformity was revealed in the glow of light. Snapping the spears protruding from its body it roared in agony. Terrified, the villagers thrust the torches into its flesh and setting it alight they fled, hearing the screams echoing from the cave.

They fled along the mountain path slipping and falling and crying out in terror.

As they looked back, they saw the creature appear at the mouth of the cave. A burning inferno that glowed in the darkness like the flames of Naraka, it stood, falling here and there until all form had gone and only a black and charred heap of smoking flesh lay smouldering in the darkness.

Breathless, the elders stood, their faces covered in blood. Thunder rolled down the valley and the monsoon unleashed a torrent of rain which flooded the mountains and deafened the ears.

As if compelled, their eyes were forced back to the cave, and from the charred remains of the monster there rose a creature, as if ascending from water, iridescent blue with many arms, her right foot placed upon the flesh dissolving beneath her foot.

Her eyes of rage bore down upon the villagers, and they fled and disappeared into the wind.

'Kali! Kali! Kali!!'

2. CHANCERY LANE. LONDON.

Some months later.

It was a cold, crisp February morning as Edward Rudgwick, a junior partner in Malbraid, Syrett and Barkworth, a respected law firm, walked into the narrow lane which led to his office.

He arrived at eight of the clock, sharp, as he had always done. But today the snow beneath his feet leant a certain serenity to the morning. A calmness he had rarely felt as he arrived for another day.

He placed his key in the lock. It jammed, as it always did. He released it, flicked the key and it responded, as it always had. One day he would have it fixed, but for the moment he drew a certain pleasure from understanding the lock and its ways and this pleased him.

As he opened the door, which creaked a familiar greeting, cold blasts of air brushed passed his face, and like children rushing out to play they danced and twirled in their greeting of the wind which whistled down the lane and carried snowflakes playing chase, until all was quiet, save for a distant bell.

It was a fine morning.

He placed his hat and coat upon the rack and put his gloves on the hallway sideboard. The mail in the little cage behind the letterbox had fallen in a perfect pyramid. Retrieving it, he climbed the stairs to his office, keeping his muffler on until he had lit the fire, and opened the shutters to let the morning light into the dark and dusty room.

Pulling his chair up to his desk he arranged the letters, as he always did, in order of date and size and flicked through each, muttering an acknowledgment of their suspected contents.

One small letter caught his attention. It was of faded yellow and its postmark was Bombay, India. He slid his paper knife along the envelope, a knife bequeathed to him by his senior partner who had retired and which he treasured. It was of fine silver with an ivory handle and lay like a dear and slumbering child in a beautifully engraved oblong casket of highly polished amboyna wood with the initials R.M on the lid.

Ranulph Malbraid. A gift from his senior partner, before he was knighted.

Slitting the envelope with the precision of a scalpel and removing the letter with care, he detected a faint aroma of spices as he read its contents.

'Mmm,' he mused.

Walking into an adjoining room, where row upon row of dusty files lined the shelves, he pulled on the white cotton gloves hanging from the hook. Inhaling the airless smell of ancient parchment as it tickled his nostrils, he ran his finger along the fragile documents, each arranged meticulously in alphabetical order.

He came upon the file he had been seeking in the section marked 'F'.

Carefully removing it, as if its contents contained the delicate and fragile dreams of the deceased, he placed it on his desk and slowly turned the dark-stained and brittle pages.

'Mmmm... Interesting, ' he muttered. 'Very interesting, indeed.'

3. ST JAMES. LONDON.

The hansom cab arrived a little after two. The normal clatter of horseshoe and wheels on the black cobbles was muffled gently by the fallen snow and straw that the hospital opposite had considerately strewn on the road to protect the sensibilities of their patients.

Rudgwick discarded his blanket and stepped down into the cold wind, which blew along the street carrying the steam from horses' nostrils and the faint aroma of horse manure - a smell, which, surprisingly, he never found offensive.

He paid the driver, adjusted his muffler, and walked up the steps to the imposing front door of the club, which seemed to open as if magically, unbidden, by an unseen doorman whose white glove grasped the highly polished brass handle and invited him in.

Leaving his cane, hat, muffler and coat, he walked across the impressive entrance hall and made his way along the plushly carpeted corridor, the walls adorned with fine paintings of long deceased members, each with the same austere expression of someone who had lived a good life, deserving of respect, but whose eyes seemed to say that... time... the hunter and final victor, finds us all.

The sounds of closing doors assured him he was in another world. The smell of pipe and cigar smoke carried on the breeze was considerably preferable to that of decaying flesh from the death carts that trundled through the back streets, reminding him that mortality, frail and fleeting, is at the mercy of each passing breath.

He found Sir Ranulph Malbraid, the senior partner and doyen of the law establishment, in the smoking room asleep in his favourite chair by a roaring fire; a cigar slowly burning between his fingers, the length of ash which clung precariously to it indicating he had been asleep for some time. Rudgwick removed it gently and placed it in the ashtray to die gracefully.

Sir Ranulph was a tall portly man, well advanced in years and the proud possessor of an elegantly trimmed grey beard. He had begun the practice forty or so years before and, with diligence and patience, had crafted it into a well-respected firm deserving of its reputation and the success it enjoyed.

His other two partners were sadly deceased, and Sir Ranulph was now a sleeping partner. Literally.

He had wisely passed on the day to day running of the practice to Rudgwick some eighteen months before, as his eyesight was fading and his concentration was on the wane, but he insisted he be consulted on anything of importance should it arise.

Rudgwick considered this case to be worthy of his considerable experience and, as he had made the original arrangements, thought it fitting that he should advise as to the best way to proceed.

He ordered a glass of Claret and warmed himself by the fire.

~

He sat for nearly an hour as the room reverberated to the sound of contented snoring and the ticking of the grandfather clock, which stood majestically by the window and was bequeathed by a distinguished member in gratitude.

Not in gratitude to the club but in gratitude to the previous clock, which had prevented him from being hit by a rock thrown from the street by rioters after missing the Duke of Wellington in his carriage, and but for the clock it would certainly have hit him in the head, which by all accounts was the gentleman's least vulnerable spot. The rock had smashed the glass and damaged the mechanism, rendering it dysfunctional, as well as badly splintering the wooden case.

The club, to their credit, had offered to replace the clock, but he was of a mind that good fortune should be rewarded, feeling it would be a timely reminder and suitable legacy for his gratitude to an establishment that had shielded him during an acrimonious divorce and allowed him to live in anonymity; thus, preserving his elite manhood as an unrepentant Bon Viveur.

The new clock was a fine specimen and had been made by John Walker of Newcastle-upon-Tyne, and bought at auction for £3.13s 6d.

The old clock had been gifted to the hospital opposite, who were less than grateful as they complained it constantly kept waking the patients.

The new clock was installed with much pomp and ceremony, but during the lavish celebrations the gentleman fatally collapsed in a chair and, after several sounds had emanated from his nether regions, which needs no explanation, he departed for the Elysium fields - one hoped.

Out of sympathy and respect, the chair had never been sat in since, as a reminder of the inevitability that the Grim Reaper, hourglass in hand, awaits us all.

After a few sniffs and snorts, Sir Ranulph emerged from the depths of his slumber and slowly began to focus on the visitor who sat opposite him.

'Oh. Hello Rudgwick,' he said, adjusting himself in his chair and trying to bring some life back to his arm, which had fallen asleep and felt like a haberdasher's cushion.

'Have you been here long?'

'Only a few minutes, Sir.'

'Judging from your almost empty glass and the ash from my cigar, which has seemingly developed legs and found its way to the ashtray, I surmise at least an hour.'

'No matter, Sir. Your powers of observation are undiminished.'

'Is this a visit for pleasure or business?'

'It is always a pleasure to see you, Sir - but, yes, also for business.'

'Please proceed. I am refreshed. 'He ordered another glass of Claret. 'Would you care to join me?'

'Thank you, no.'

He finished what remained in his glass and placed it carefully on the table beside him.

‘I must ask you to cast your mind back several decades Sir, to a matter concerning one Lieutenant Colonel Sir Henry Faulkner. Reported missing. Presumed dead.’

Sir Ranulph's demeanour changed to one of sombre and melancholy reflection.

‘It is a case I shall never forget. A truly courageous man, and a very sad story.’

He sat up in his chair and stared intently into the fire, collecting his thoughts like the barrister he was, before giving his final address to the jury.

He continued.

‘He was part of the first assault at the battle of Isandlwana against the Zulu kingdom. A humiliating defeat for us and brought about mainly by hubris and incompetence on the part of the commanding officers.

A junior officer in his regiment was badly wounded. He dismounted and tried to lift the man onto his horse and bring him to safety, but as the Zulus in their thousands advanced, in the mayhem, they were hit by friendly fire.

The impact blew half of his face away and robbed him of an arm. Had the horse not taken the full impact of the blast he would almost certainly have not survived. He was left during the retreat and was presumed dead.'

His claret arrived and was placed on the silver tray on the small table at his side.

'Thank you, Barker.'

'My pleasure, Sir.'

'Missing for several days, he eventually turned up in a state of delirium. Miraculously he had survived. He was found, barely alive, outside a temporary military hospital at night, laying on a bed of white feathers and covered in a Zulu shield. They had honoured his bravery. Not quite the savages the British had imagined.

After several alarming months and with the tenderest of care he recovered, but his injuries were horrific.'

'Did he return to England?' asked Rudgwick.

'No. His family were all connected to the military and went back several generations. He was perhaps burdened a little by personal pride and tormented that he could be of no further service to the Empire.

He wrote to me, as I had always handled the affairs of his estate, and explained that as he was so badly disfigured, he had no desire to subject his family to the grotesqueness of his injuries and would not be able to endure the daily displays of pity, however well intentioned, and so wished to remain missing in action. Presumed dead.'

'Was he mentally unstable?'

'One would have thought so, but his letter to me was remarkably coherent and he was quite precise about his wishes.'

Sir Ranulph sipped at his Claret.

'He was posthumously awarded the Victoria Cross for bravery in the field. It was upsetting to see his family collect it on his behalf, knowing he was still alive, but... those were his instructions. When he had fully recovered, I believe he travelled to India where he had leased a small coal mine in the mountains. He hoped he could live in peace, anonymity, and solitude.'

'Your memory serves you well, Sir. I'm sorry to report that I received a letter from Bombay this morning regrettably informing me of his death. Apparently, he committed suicide.'

Malbraid stared for a long time into the flames, his normally congenial expression now one of deep sadness.

'If that is true, and we should investigate, it does not surprise me. The extent of his injuries must have led to a challenging life.

Malbraid reached into his pocket and removed his Faux-Blonde cigar case. Rubbing his hand over its tortoise shell covering, he carefully pushed the silver button and opening it, removed another cigar - easily, as the straps had long since disintegrated.

He would not normally indulge in two cigars at lunchtime but as the last one had finished without his assistance, he felt less selfish, and was in need of comfort.

He clicked the case shut and was always surprised that he found such a simple sound so satisfying. He snipped the end of the fine cigar and offered up a naked flame, puffing gentle wisps of smoke which ascended slowly to the mists which already hung below the wooden ornate ceiling like a Himalayan cloud in the Hindu Kush.

The carved ceiling already bore the signs of sepia-staining reminiscent of the ones at Eton, where generations of small boys had once been encouraged to smoke a pipe before breakfast for their health and to ward off worms and halitosis. Indeed, they were beaten soundly if they did not.

But thankfully the curse of Hawkins, Raleigh and the deadly leaf had faded into obscurity when he was a pupil there; however, the habit of a good cigar, almost a ceremony, always lifted his spirits and improved his sense of well-being, despite the concerns of the medical faculty who persisted with the ridiculous notion that it was bad for your health. But, as potatoes were once considered dangerous, opinions can change in a heartbeat. So let it be.

Emerging from his reverie he continued.

‘There were instructions I recall in the agreement that in the event of his demise I was to travel to where he was, obtain proof of death and to make the arrangements necessary to pass over any remaining funds to his family from an anonymous donor. Obviously, I am now too old to embark on such an enterprise, so you must make the journey for me Rudgwick.’

‘But... I have rarely ventured outside of London, Sir,' said Rudgwick, somewhat alarmed at the prospect.

'Then let it be an education for you. Travel has the quality of changing one's essence. It can be a revelation to see ourselves through other's eyes. The British Empire is not the centre of the world, Rudgwick, although we misguidedly think it is.'

‘As you wish, Sir. I shall leave in a few days, which will give my letter a head start, informing them of my arrival.'

‘Excellent and that will give me time to release the funds that were provided in the will for this... undertaking.’

He smiled cynically at his unintended slip of the tongue. Settling back in his chair, he gave a deep sigh.

'What an unfortunate ending, for such an extraordinary man.'

4. BERLIN.

The snow was lying deep on the ground as Frau Bergmeier alighted from the tram in Hackescher Markt and made her way to the small café where she met her friend every Saturday morning before their afternoon concert, to plan their adventures for the next day. Frau Bergmeier normally played first violin and her dearest friend Frau Köehler would normally play second violin. But truth to tell, there was nothing normal about either of these remarkable women, who had formed an unbreakable bond over many years of sitting near to each other in the front rows of their orchestra in Berlin and tours around Europe. Indeed, they were often mistaken for sisters, both possessing the most beautiful blond hair tied back in Germanic plaits and having the most alluring blue eyes, which when they gazed at you made you feel you were the only person in the world they would rather be talking to. Coupled with an intellect as sharp as a Prussian sword and a wit worthy of the Wanderbühne you were indeed fortunate to enjoy their company.

As Frau Bergmeier approached the café she could not see if her friend had yet arrived as the windows were so steamed up with condensation, and only saw her sitting at their corner window table, which they always reserved, as she entered.

Frau Köehler looked up as the bell on the door jingled and waved to her friend.

'Good morning, Frau Köehler.'

'Good morning, Frau Bergmeier.'

They had always greeted each other in this formal way, it was a form of affection and respect that they both enjoyed and was often the subject of amusement to their colleagues in the orchestra.

'And how are you today, Frau Köehler?'

'Extremely well thank you, Frau Bergmeier. And you?'

'Enjoying the best of health and somewhat excited Frau Köehler.'

'Oh, and why is that, may I ask?'

'Allow me first to order my coffee and light my cigarette, and I will tell you.'

After Frau Bergmeier's coffee arrived, she removed her gloves, cupped it in her hands, and enjoying the warmth in her palms, gently sipped at the frothy chocolate which laced the top of the cup.

Lighting her cigarette, she enjoyed the rush of smoke to her lungs, which seemed to empower her.

'Now,' said Frau Bergmeier, placing the hot beverage on the table to one side and taking Frau Köehler's hand. 'I have wonderful news!'

'Which is?'

'As you are aware, we have discussed my promised sabbatical. I have spoken with the leader, and he assures me that as long as I am able to find suitable substitutes of the highest quality, I am allowed to leave next weekend.' She sat back beaming with delight. 'For a year!'

'Goodness.'

'Not only that, but he has also agreed, and this is the cause of my excitement, that you may accompany me.'

'Goodness.'

'So, I have purchased two tickets to Bombay, India, at my expense and we leave next Sunday!'

'Sunday?'

'Yes.'

'But... why me, Frau Bergmeier?'

Frau Bergmeier placed her cigarette in the ashenbecker and took her friend's hand.

'My dear Frau Köehler, if you cannot understand why I would not embark on such an exciting journey without my dearest friend by my side, then you have not the slightest inkling of the affection in which I hold you.'

Frau Köehler removed her glasses and wiped her eyes with her napkin.

'Well, I never.'

'So, will you come?'

She smiled shyly.

'Most assuredly.'

5. TO SOUTHAMPTON.

A week later, Rudgwick made his way to Nine Elms station. He had sensibly sent his luggage ahead to make the journey less tiresome and was catching an earlier train than needed to be confident of arriving with sufficient composure.

The train to Southampton was slow and the journey arduous but the countryside, once you left London, was pleasant enough when you were able to glimpse it through the engine smoke.

Rudgwick was unfamiliar with the country, having spent his entire life in the confines of London, save for an occasional visit to the suburbs to lay flowers on his parents' grave.

He pulled down the window and was rewarded by a rush of air. Looking out at the fields as they passed at Basingstoke, the snow had melted, and he found the predominance of green meadows, trees and the distant bells from country spires, even in winter, comforting and healing, and determined to spend more time in the future exploring beyond the city.

He sat back down in his seat and tried to ease the rigid starched collar, which felt like a tourniquet on his neck. The gentle clatter of the train over the rails was hypnotic and its rhythm slowly rocked him off to sleep.

In the hushed realms of slumber, amidst the rhythmic lullaby of the iron steed, Rudgwick found himself ensconced in a peculiar limbo betwixt consciousness and dreams.

The carriage, a cocoon of warmth and gentle sways, cradled its somnolent occupants with a gentle tenderness reminiscent of infancy.

Through half closed eyes, the plumes of smoke, wisps of ephemeral reverie, danced outside the window, taking on ethereal forms that waltzed with the dawn shadows.

In this state between wakefulness and the embrace of Morpheus, the imagination paints an impressionistic picture upon the canvas of the mind. The clinking wheels metamorphose into the measured footsteps of unseen phantoms, marching to the cadence of a spectral parade. Imagination unfurls its wings, the mundane becomes magical, and the mechanical becomes a fantastical menagerie of the mind.

The clickety-clack of the iron track becomes the heartbeat of an ancient giant, a slumbering titan whose dreams echo through the caverns of time.

As the train hurtled towards its destination, Rudgwick navigated this delicate boundary, savouring the transient splendour of this half-waking interlude, that mysterious realm where reality and fantasy coexist in harmonious discord.

~

Southampton Harbour.

Rudgwick had assured Sir Ranulph on several occasions that he did not expect the same level of comfort the worthy gentleman would have demanded had he been young enough to make the voyage, but his protestations were

dismissed, and Sir Ranulph insisted that he should enjoy the same attention to detail and luxury as himself, to make the journey less arduous.

Sir Ranulph possessed no children, and any relatives had long since departed. So, even though it was never mentioned, Rudgwick thought he rather regarded him as the son he never had, or at least a beloved nephew. Certainly, he did not spoil or indulge him; however, on this occasion, Sir Ranulph felt that as a representative of the company he should present himself in as good a light as possible. To that end, he had opened an account at Ede & Ravenscroft in Burlington Gardens with instructions that he should be furnished with a wardrobe befitting the impending climate.

As the majority of their clientele were perhaps larger than most, indulging their well-earned wealth, the slimmer clothes were more readily available and with a little nipping and tucking could be ready well before his departure.

And now, in the comfort of his cabin, Rudgwick carefully hung his new clothes on the highly polished hangers and placed his crisp new shirts still wrapped in monogrammed paper in the fine mahogany chest, admiring the beautiful fruitwood inlay decorating the front of the deep draws. A world away from the simple solid desks and musky wooden shelves of his office in Chancery Lane.

Indeed, it was a fine cabin. On the port side it gave him an uninterrupted view of the sea from its portal, which was splendidly encased in highly polished burnished brass which shone magnificently.The Mahogany wood-panelling leant the whole cabin an air of opulence which, truth to tell, he found a little intimidating.

Once the remainder of his luggage had been unloaded and stored in his cabin, Rudgwick went up on deck in an effort to rid himself of the smell of coal dust and smoke on his clothes. Catching an earlier train meant he was able to settle calmly.

He watched the passengers and crew bustling on the quayside, trying to avoid the horses and carriages bringing hordes of passengers. Some who did not come with staff scrambled for a porter and looked indignant that they should have to queue to be allowed up the gangplank.

Years of punctuality had served him well, and the knowledge that as a rule people did not behave well under stress made him avoid it whenever possible.

It would be a few hours before the ship departed, docking first in Bremen and then onwards to the next port of call. He had studied the itinerary well.

Depending on whether provisions on board were running low, it may have been necessary to dock at the Cape of Good Hope or the Port of Aden. Either way, it would be a long voyage and one could only pray that it did not fall foul of bad weather or illness. Several months at sea was not a prospect he was relishing, but needs must; it was little discomfort, considering what the client had gone through and his unfortunate demise, which made him feel even more uncomfortable, guilty to be enjoying such luxuriant surroundings at his expense.

~

The coming weeks at sea would show the behavioural habits of people in a confined space. Slowly the routine settled, and they began to spend time with passengers they felt comfortable with and inevitably avoided those they had an instant and usually unfounded distrust of.

Introductions took their time but, being creatures of habit, they would sit in a favourite chair and enjoy a polite nod in acknowledgment of their fellow travellers before finding a suitable moment to break the ice. Those precious first moments that would either draw them together or make them retreat behind that polished British veneer.

As many different nationalities had joined the ship at various ports, there was at least that enjoyable and interesting custom of getting to know another culture and hopefully presenting yourself as a good ambassador for your nation. There was of course the occasional passenger who would run down his own country to ingratiate himself, but, as a general rule, this was confined to the insecure, uneducated and jejune - and was somewhat frowned upon.

6. BOMBAY. DAWN.

It was shortly after dawn had awoken that Doctor Surinda climbed into his cart and made his way to the harbour.

Remaining waters from the monsoon seeped into the earth and caked the wheels in mud. The mist, like spirits creeping home to rest, passed in the jungle, and gentle sap from the tired trees, verdant from the recent torrent, dripped slowly from the leaves. A passing scent of sweet rotting fruits and morning air filled his nostrils , which made him shiver. Wrapping a light blanket around his shoulders to warm his old bones, he urged the oxen onwards down the jungle path.

Only the occasional early birdsong broke the silence.

The northeast monsoon had rained for months washing homes and habitats away with the floods.

'They are too busy rebuilding nests to worry about singing yet,' he chuckled.

He rode out through the paddy fields, which stretched across the hills like a turquoise carpet in the early light, and thin wisps of blood red clouds hung in the quiet sky.

Before him stretched the sprawling city of Bombay and the harbour beyond.

It would be sometime before he reached the outskirts. He would leave his cart with Raj, his friend, and walk to the harbour and while he was gone his friend would wash down the wheels, feed the oxen and, when he returned, they would take morning tea together.

He lifted his parcel from the seat and brushed the dried pine needles to the floor; a gift of fresh white linen, fruit, and money for the temple to bless his journey.

At the hotel he would confirm the rooms. Even though it would be at least a few months before the ship arrived, he wanted to make sure that everything was in readiness for his visitors; arranging food that would be more suitable to their taste.

7. THE VOYAGE CONTINUES.

The duchess entered the elegant saloon and looked around for a suitable chair that would support her considerable posterior.

Having selected an acceptable perch, she lowered herself into the plushness of its leather with the dexterity of a shifting crane. Placing her glasses onto her nose she surveyed the room with a beaming smile as if each occupant was solely there for her pleasure.

‘Well! Isn't this lovely!’ she bellowed, with the confidence of one who is used to putting others at their ease but achieving the opposite effect. ‘Now, who are you, and where are you from?'

Her eyes fell on the two ladies sitting opposite her.

‘I am Frau Bergmeier, and this is my dearest friend Frau Köehler. We are violinists with the Philharmonischer Orchestra in Berlin.’

‘Oh yes! How very courageous of you all! To form another orchestra! How exciting! You must be delighted you are no longer at the mercy of Mr Bilse. With the added benefit, no doubt, that you will no longer have to travel fourth class.’

She smiled, and her two cheeks shone like apples in the sun.

Frau Bergmeier was surprised at the knowledge the duchess possessed and looked forward to an entertaining and no doubt enlightening voyage.

‘We had already planned to put in substitutes before the last orchestra was disbanded,’ said Frau Köehler shyly. ‘And so, they graciously honoured our request.’

‘How polite of you to call it an orchestra, my dear. It was a band when I saw it in Paris,’ she laughed loudly but not unkindly.

‘Frau Köehler blushed, sipped her wine, and returned to the book she was reading.

‘And who is this handsome young man may I ask!?’

Rudgwick stiffened in his chair.

‘I am Edward Rudgwick of Malbraid, Syrett and Barkworth. A respected law firm in Chancery Lane. London. And I am travelling on business.’

‘How exciting! What kind of business?’

‘Regrettably, due to client confidentiality I am unable to enlighten you further.’

‘I quite understand, Mr Rudgwick, although I will find you out,' replied the duchess, teasingly. 'I have my ways. I have elves that work for me,’ she giggled.

Rudgwick looked slightly uncomfortable but smiled shyly and settled back in his chair.

‘Perhaps,’ she suggested,’ you may encounter a romantic liaison, or two, Mr Rudgwick.’ Her eyes mischievously darting between her two newly acquainted German companions.

Rudgwick looked slightly alarmed and Frau Köehler peered over the top of her book, the collected poems of Baudelaire. Les Fleurs du Mal.

'And judging from Frau Köehler's choice of literature I suspect she may be of a similar mind.'

Frau Bergmeier let out a laugh that seemed to reverberate around the saloon, much to the consternation of her travelling companion who blushed profusely, clumsily stuffing her book back in her purse.

'Ah, it is a tragedy,' the duchess continued, 'that one must die in agony, induced by opium, poverty and public indecency before we can discover, that heart, that flutters like a fledgling bird.'

The saloon fell silent.

A common thought seemed to permeate the room that no one had asked the purpose of the duchess's visit - or, indeed who she was - but no doubt they would be enlightened later. And so they were.

A rather large gentlemen playing cards at a nearby table turned in frustration.

'Good heavens! Are we to be subjected to this endless babble every evening woman?!'

The duchess smiled sweetly and, like someone who had carefully crafted her armour plating, replied, 'Well, there is a remedy, dear sir. You could sit in one of the other saloons - there are several - and that way you would be spared your irritation. In the meantime, may I suggest a laxative?'

The gentleman seemed to choke on his port and stormed out, his red face about to explode and uttering a cacophony of words that bore no resemblance to any known language.

'Oh dear. Now I must see him at breakfast every morning for the next few months.'

'I think the gentleman deserved your just repost,' suggested Frau Bergmeier, laughing.

'Unfortunately, those are the very men we must face in the future to achieve equality, my dear, and mine was a perfect example of how not to approach the challenge. My failing is, I never reproach myself. I find there are so many more who are willing and better qualified to do it for me.'

'But you live to tell the tale,' said Frau Köehler. 'I wish I possessed your courage.'

8. ROUNDING THE CAPE OF GOOD HOPE.

West of Aden.

Frau Bergmeier and Frau Köehler relaxed in the sleeper chairs they favoured on the main deck, which afforded them some much needed shade but didn't stop the warming sun from filtering through the deck canopies.

The days were long and sometimes tedious. Relationships formed and dissolved, as changeable as the weather, and like water found their own level. Even sunsets became banal, like an excess of confectionery.

Somehow the small group remained pleasant travelling companions. They read each other's' books and spent many an interesting evening exchanging opinions. Simple games on deck or an attempt at a painting received polite encouragement or dismissive grunts, and all passed the time. A game of bridge or chess, and a pipe or cigar would add a certain serenity to an after-dinner conversation.

As they neared the Port of Aden, the Indian Ocean beckoned where the Ten Commandments lose their voice, and lazy days were spent in steamer chairs reading out-of-date newspapers and magazines, or idly watching silhouettes that passed across the sun. Frau Bergmeier sipped at her lemonade, brought by one of the obliging stewards, who, for some inexplicable reason, were all called Buxton; either not to tax the memories of the ageing passengers, or some private joke shared only amongst the waiting staff.

Frau Bergmeier glimpsed up at the afternoon sun through half-closed eyes.

The shape, lines and colours of form seemed to blur into a sparkling hue and an epiphany of art danced in the light like diamonds on her eyelashes.

Lost in a migraine of Gauguinesque reverie she watched the ocean gently ripple; the way that oil might ripple; the way that blood might ripple; shimmering, thick, congealed. A warm and sensuous feeling made her slender body melt as if her blood had turned to nectar.

Restless passengers, convinced that something would have changed on their monotonous perambulations, sauntered by; their polite greetings at morning noon and night gave way to tired nods as they passed.

Dressing for dinner became less formal, as collars and corsets seemed out of place in the relentless heat.

Once the constraints of attire were dispensed with, it affected even the most proper of persons. It relaxed laughter and a sense of contented freedom permeated the ship.

Only the captain and crew remained in full dress and livery throughout the voyage, except for the occasional dalliance and clandestine meeting with a crew member in a female cabin, where the laborious wait of removing layer upon layer of garments was rewarded by a surge of passion and frustrated complaints from the adjoining cabins.

As the days sailed by, they felt the restrictions of their daily lives in Europe fall away. Although sometimes a valued burden, they were happy to be free of their constraints and felt a gradual warmth descending like the thoughts and

feelings released on a summer's day that had been hidden in the winter's frost; an iceberg in the sun changing form, changing essence.

That afternoon, to the group's surprise and delight, they each received a personal card of invitation from the duchess to be her guest at dinner that evening and requesting a short concert be played afterwards, if they were agreeable and had brought their instruments.

To be in the presence of such a distinguished guest filled them all with excitement and anticipation, so they decided to dress for dinner out of respect.

9. AN INVITATION FROM THE DUCHESS.

The dining room was exquisite and the ocean calm, so the chandeliers did not swing erratically. There was a murmur of excitement amongst the Buxtons in the room that the guests had dressed for dinner, feeling that standards had not completely slipped.

The duchess was already seated at the table when the guests arrived.

The meal was memorable, and the cuisine infinitely better than the restaurant they were familiar with.

At the arrival of the brandy, the duchess told them that they may smoke if they wished.

'A favourite game of mine,' confessed the duchess, 'is to ask what person in history would you have liked to have met, and why? I will begin.

Dante!

Now, I firmly believe that Dante should be removed from the educational curriculum, especially those preparing for a political career. And as it is said he put his friends in Heaven and his enemies in Hell he was, perhaps, a little biassed in his judgments. Also, whilst no doubt a brilliant poet, his view of women is far too myopic. We are neither purely virginal angels nor duplicitous Machiavellian seductresses. Discuss.'

One by one, they presented their favoured historical figure. The conversation was amusing and sometimes electric.

'So often these ancient figureheads have shaped our modern thinking, and it is necessary we understand whether their impact is still relevant, and which should be taken with a large pinch of the mineral so beautifully encased in this silver condiment.'

She held up an exquisitely engraved salt seller.

'I remember,' continued the duchess, 'when returning from America, there was a fancy dress ball in the Grand Saloon. It was magical. It was where I met my husband, who was suffering from a bad bout of sea sickness, which seemed perfectly in keeping with his Pierrot costume. He was as white as a sheet, poor man.

Women are strange creatures.' she laughed. 'We fall in love with men when they are at their most vulnerable!'

A pleasant silence fell, ended by eight strikes of the ship's bell. She was glad they had decided to dine early, although they were the last group left in the dining room.

The duchess looked affectionately at her new acquaintances.

They moved to the window seats where they could see a spectacular display of stars in the night sky.

'When I meet people who I think are genuinely compassionate,' said the duchess, 'to solidify our friendship, I ask that they reveal something about which they feel vulnerable. This is by no means to exploit their confidences but to bring us closer. There will be no judgement, and no comment, and of course if you do not wish to, I shall not compel you.'

The guests fell silent in contemplation.

Surprisingly, it was Frau Köehler who spoke first.

'I had a very lonely childhood. It came from the misperceptions of a small child. There were many uneducated people who lived nearby, and my parents would write the letters to their creditors to help them. They resented having to ask them, so to somehow assuage their shame and dependence they secretly made their children exclude me. I of course knew nothing of this. I grew up believing I was not likeable.'

Frau Bergmeier gently took her hand.

The next to speak was Rudgwick who had remained standing to stretch his legs.

'When my parents died, I was left with sufficient money to be given a fine education. In my chosen school there was a very obnoxious fellow who bullied and terrified everyone. And soon his attention fell to me.

I was a very thin undernourished child, so one day, when I knew he was leaving a lecture, I climbed to the top of the corridor bookcase and tucking several very large books under my arms I fell on him, breaking his arm and his spirit - rendering him unconscious.

He never knew how it had happened, but believed it was some kind of divine justice from above.

My school days from that day forth were a delight and I flourished, but I have always carried with me the shame that I could not find a more intelligent way of dealing with his injustice.

I believe it was Abraham Lincoln who said, "I don't like that man. I must get to know him better."

Surprisingly the boy in question later left the law school and entered the clergy.'

The duchess smiled reassuringly and considered for a moment just how honest she wished to be.

'The late duke, my husband, was a very weak man. He was born into a military establishment and his father was a much-decorated war hero. His two brothers followed in his father's footsteps, but it was always a dilemma as to what they would do with their younger brother, who had an intense dislike of confrontation. His father was a hunter and spent many a time shooting in Alaska and Africa. Several of his trophies hung on the castle walls. There was a massive moose whose antlers spread twelve feet across the entrance hall which he'd brought back from Alaska, and a huge gorilla head from Africa which hung above the toilet outside my husband's bedroom when he was a child. Terrified, he would wet the bed rather than venture into the dark corridor at night.

When we met, he needed constant validation of his confidence, which being of a strong nature I felt I was able to give him. Indeed, I relished being able to give him that support. But eventually as the years passed, I grew frustrated at his inability to help himself and to my shame I withdrew to my parents' house in Scotland. I was exhausted both physically and spiritually, and had nothing left to give.

Eventually, he drank himself to death.

Beware of the leech .It masquerades as a lame duck and when it has drained you of compassion and you are an empty shell, it will die. Leaving you guilty and bereft.'

For a moment, she was lost in thought.

'Do you know the leech anaesthetizes you when it bites? The way dependent people do with false love.

That may sound harsh, but I do not believe he ever loved me. only... needed me. There are quite simply some people who are beyond even the tenderest of help.'

Frau Bergmeier took out a cigarette and was plainly distressed. She lit it and, after a few minutes said, 'my father... my father... forgive me.'

She fell silent.

There was a tender melancholy in her face. A fleeting vulnerability that no one spoke of, but all had witnessed, and for a brief moment the sadness in her silence was palpable. A graveyard of shattered dreams lay bare before them.

The duchess, Carpe Diem, rose from her chair assisted by two obliging Buxtons. 'But we move forward!' she bellowed, 'with an indomitable spirit because our children need us.'

She retrieved her purse from the table.

'My daughter once declared that when she grew up, she wanted to be Queen of the world .I asked her what she thought the Queen actually did. She considered this a while and said, "The Queen gets up in the morning, puts on her golden knickers... and reigns!"

How wonderfully simple things seem in childhood. And so, they should.

My son despised the world and wished to destroy it. All I could do was create a space where he could hate safely, and I could nurse his paranoia that everyone thought him an incorrigible fellow. Until that inevitable road to Damascus when we realise how many people there are who actually never think about us at all, and our disappointment gives rise to an awakening. We hope.'

Buxton placed her shawl around her shoulders.

'Thank you. And now, if you are willing, perhaps we may enjoy the promised musical soiree, shall we adjourn to the saloon?'

She glanced across at Frau Bergmeier whose face bore witness to a grief she had not resolved and gently taking her arm she carefully led her from the room.

The group walked along the promenade deck to the saloon, avoiding an energetic game of quoits, played by some over-inebriated passengers.

The moon was full and a welcome evening breeze blew across the ship.

'Ah, what it is to be young and carefree. Before the burdens of family life fill our days with worry and wonder,' said the duchess.

'Do you hope to marry one day, Frau Bergmeier?' said Rudgwick.

'It may shock you to know that I have already been married, Mr Rudgwick. I am a widow. But... that is a story for another time... perhaps. But am I not human, Mr Rudgwick? Do I not have needs? Desires? I hope as someone with a beating heart and blood in my veins I will be allowed to seek fulfilment and not languish in a barren life. For is it the lot of my sex that I must wait for a man to want me before my life can begin, that I am somehow incomplete? Do you suppose that being prisoners of the age and denied the full expression of our womanhood, that it is so easily laid aside and devalued? I hope to find a man who will see me as an equal.'

'Perhaps... it might be better to have higher aspirations,' said Rudgwick, shyly.

She laughed.

'But equality will benefit us all. It should be a right for every person, don't you think? Human rights have no gender, in politics or love.'

'We should all be part of the body politic, should we not my dear?' said the duchess, whacking a drunken passenger who had stumbled across her path with her cane.

'I agree,' replied Frau Bergmeier, 'and if you stem the flow of blood for too long, Mr Rudgwick, the whole body suffers. And who knows what passions may surface from the depths of the hidden heart, what tender sensuality may be released as we're removed from polite constraints.'

Rudgwick found himself becoming uncomfortable. He was not used to the company of women and found them alluring but unsettling, so decided to withdraw to a distance where he could observe from a position of safety.

Frau Bergmeier was an attractive woman and Rudgwick felt surprisingly and uncharacteristically confused.

'I have offended you, Mr Rudgwick. It was not my intention, but I feel passionately that we could be of so much more use to you than merely gracing your beds,' she smiled reassuringly, and added, 'as enjoyable as we might find it.'

Frau Köehler was shocked and blushed profusely. 'Frau Bergmeier!' she gasped.

'Not at all' said Rudgwick. 'I am still a young man and not so knowledgeable about the ways of the world. In a profession that only seeks justice and the truth, fact and not fiction, we can be a little 'book headed', as my senior partner would say. I find you enlightening, and I am sure I will find this voyage educational.'

They entered the saloon.

Frau Bergmeier was pleasantly surprised that her frank outburst had not alienated the young man, who despite her best intentions was becoming more and more attractive to her.

'That was a very diplomatic reply, Mr Rudgwick,' she said warmly.

'When I was in Paris recently,' said the duchess,' there was a young female writer. Oh dear, I forget her name. A visionary. I believe her writing will become important in the future. In time we will be gifted the vote.'

Frau Bergmeier laughed warmly.

'I'm sure that is the way our male colleagues will frame it,' she said 'but it will be a demand. Not a gift.'

'Evolution is preferable to revolution my dear. It gives society time to adjust, without bloodshed.'

In deference to her elder, Frau Bergmeier fell silent.

‘I am so glad,’ the duchess continued, changing the subject ‘that you have brought your instruments with you and we are to enjoy a soiree after dinner.’

‘Indeed, we have.’ said Frau Köehler. ‘Sadly, we do not have a pianist, or the evening might have been more enjoyable.’

Rudgwick glanced across at her.

‘Although by no means proficient… I am able to play a little.’

‘Mr Rudgwick,’ said Frau Bergmeier, gazing at him.

‘I find myself pleasantly surprised that you not only possess the qualities of a diplomat but also the accomplishment of an artist.'

‘And I become more and more impressed at your mastery of the English language.’

They both smiled affectionately at each other, and all could see a flame had been lit.

~

Frau Bergmeier produced the sheet music and placed it on the piano.

‘Pachelbel. Canon in D major,’ said Rudgwick. ‘A beautiful piece. I hope I will do it justice.’

They began to play. All in the saloon sat entranced, and felt so privileged to be there at that time and in that place.

When the short piece was over, there was much applause and eager requests for more. Eventually, the evening drew to a close.

'Music is such a balm to the soul,' said Rudgwick, quite moved by the emotion stirred within him.

'It has the power to change one's very essence, Mr Rudgwick,' said the duchess. 'Both evocative and enigmatic, it is the echo of the hidden winds of nature. The celestial structure of patterned sound.

Did you know that if you write Mozart's music down in mathematical form it is always equal, even numbers in structure? That is why it is so pleasing to the ear and why we are so uplifted by it. Whilst others, I'm sorry to say, seem to grate on the ear, seem discordant, and always transcribe as uneven numbers, and the ear recoils.

I believe I once heard it said that Bach, I think it was Bach, did a great disservice to music. By allowing us to move freely from key-to-key, musicians have been apparently playing happily out of tune ever since!

The tonic scale is not made up of equal notes, although appearing so to the human ear. Each vibrates at a different frequency I'm told. I mean... mathematically speaking.'

She seemed to drift in her reverie.

'Each note a little closer to the absolute, each scale an upward spiral to heaven, until the penultimate Judas note, where it can all come crashing down and we are returned.... to the dullness from which we rise.'

She looked around at the bewildered faces of her companions, 'but I'm rambling, as is my won't! I really am a vestibule of quite useless information.'

They all smiled at her affectionately.

Placing her violin back in its case, Frau Bergmeier and Rudgwick's eyes met across the piano. He collected the music together, but several pages fell to the carpet. Picking them up, he gave them nervously to her.

'Mr Rudgwick, would you care to join me on deck? I feel in need of a little fresh air.'

'Oh dear!' exclaimed Frau Köehler. 'Your finger appears to be bleeding, duchess.'

She looked down.

'Ah,' she thought for a moment. 'I must have pricked it on a pin left in my dress. How irritating! I do hope I shan't fall asleep for a hundred years. I have far too much to do!'

Helping Frau Bergmeier on with her cloak, Rudgwick said, 'you are both excellent violinists. Maybe one day you will be famous.'

'Fame is a fickle mistress,' said the duchess, 'and you are fortunate if she comes to you late in your life.'

'Why so?' asked Rudgwick.

'Because then you are too old and breathless to chase after her, and too wise to be dazzled by her empty promises. Contentedness is a better quest. It is a quiet gift. She makes no fanfare when she enters.'

'But I must confess in my dreams I have often wished for fame,' said Frau Köehler, blushing.

The duchess rose and smiled, placing a gentle hand on her cheek.

‘If you live in fantasy, my dear, reality will always be a disappointment.'

~

The ocean was still as they walked in silence.

Frau Bergmeier took Rudgwick's arm, and they both stood watching the moonlight on the water.

She turned to him.

‘There was much tragedy in his life. Pachelbel. He lost his first love and their child. To me, I think it shows in other characteristically melancholy pieces he composed. The loss and hope of love.’

'I am still very much a novice in those emotions,’ said Rudgwick. ‘Perhaps it is something for the future.’

She looked at him and thought how young he seemed, even though they were of a similar age. How unspoiled by life. No ruined days. As the wind played with his hair, she thought how frighteningly unprepared for life he was.

'I will let you into a secret, Mr Rudgwick. Love does not want you as you are. It must take you apart, tear by tear until...here’.

She placed a hand on his chest.

‘Where your heart once was. It finds that sad and tortured empty space and fills it with burning blood and fractured gilded mirrors where it can adore.... itself. It is a high price we pay, but pay we must if we wish to submit. But it is not elegant. Not noble. It cuts your heart like a knife and can either leave it as an un-weeded graveyard that hides from the light, or a chrysalis transformed.

No. Love does not want you as you are. It has the power to reduce you to a quivering imbecile. To leave you like a Galleon abandoned on the shore.'

She walked off along the deck and he stood transfixed at the slenderness of her body and the beauty of her face, and thought how she must have suffered once.

10. QUIET CONFIDENCES.

Frau Köehler wrapped the duchess's finger with her handkerchief to stem the flow of blood.

'Thank you, my dear. Let us hope your handkerchief has the same healing qualities as the one Christ sent to the King of Agbar in Edessa!'

Frau Köehler was somewhat lost.

'Are you sure we should not call the ship's doctor ,duchess?'

'I think not. I have since discovered that the doctor is our recent acquaintance who appeared to have a constipation problem, and who stormed out with such rudeness from the saloon last month. I think we should avoid him at all costs.'

'Is he always so rude when he meets you?'

'Oh yes.'

'But does it not annoy you?'

'Certainly not. I have no intention of allowing him to dictate the mood I shall spend the rest of my day in.

After all, if someone offers you a present and you refuse to accept it, who does it stay with?'

'Why, the person who offered it?' said Frau Köehler.

'Precisely,'

They chuckled.

‘Anyway, let us not dwell on the unfortunate. All cynics are lapsed romantics, so there may be hope for him yet.’

‘I do hope,’ continued the duchess, changing the subject, ‘that you were eventually able to leave your childhood experiences behind, and discover that you are an amiable and extremely likeable young lady?’

‘That is very kind of you. It did take many years and it was only when I had finally extricated myself from a particularly destructive relationship that I was able to gain a better perspective of life.’

‘Perhaps you can walk me to my cabin, and we can talk further. It has been a memorable evening and one I shall treasure, but I am now in need of rest.’

~

As they passed into the Indian Ocean, a tradition on the ship was a magnificent firework display and evening party.

As the evening drew in, everyone assembled aft of the ship and from a safe distance watched in awe. For a moment, the tediousness of the voyage was forgotten; a sense of relief descended that they were nearing the halfway point of their journey, and had avoided bad weather and illness.

Or, so they had thought.

11. THE TEN COMMANDMENTS FADE.

The firework display was spectacular and everyone on the ship was filled with wonder that it seemed to go on forever.

That simple pleasure of watching colour explode before their eyes, lighting up the night sky, and each new explosion brought gasps of excitement and applause.

There were no children on the ship, but in a single moment each person returned to the magic of their childhood - so often filled with memories of wonder. Memories of hope and expectation that the world would fulfil every dream promised in a bedtime story book and read by a loving parent, filling their children's heads with mystery and magic, and for a few moments helping them forget the banality of daily toil. Or the important worries that a child struggles with, before falling off to sleep into a dream where little minds journey through the labyrinths of mystery and myths bequeathed by an earlier wanderer.

The passengers looked at each other with smiles and laughter, and all felt an inexplicable bond of affection that they had witnessed something they would always treasure. A memory to recall on a cold winter's night in a country a world away.

The ship's doctor gazed up with indifference.

'Does it not please you Mr Chandler?' said the duchess.

He snorted.

'Stuff and nonsense. Complete waste of time and money,' he said.

The duchess watched him walking off alone along the deck and turning to Frau Köehler, she whispered, 'Ah. The day you can walk away from a firework display, is the day you know you have lost the magic in your life.'

Although she felt he should be awarded some credit for nurturing, in his way, the ship's passengers, and with his guidance and advice he'd prevented any unseen horrors descending on the ship, his insistence, indeed demand, for ruthless hygiene at Port Aden was advice well given and fortunately heeded.

His instruction when they first began the voyage to have "One hand for yourself, and one hand for the ship!" had prevented, no doubt, many a fall down the staircases after a drunken night of revelry.

~

There was a general feeling of excitement and anticipation on the ship that they would reach their destination in the coming weeks. Some, eager for dry land, had already packed, and the crew were busy cleaning the ship so that it shone like a new pin for when it entered the harbour in Bombay.

That evening they assembled for what was to be their last formal dinner. The duchess, much to everyone's surprise, invited Mr Chandler to sit with them and, to everyone's surprise, he accepted, but used the opportunity to be as obnoxious as possible.

‘It is perhaps,’ he bellowed, ‘one of life's bazaar injustices that we have no control about where we first open our eyes in this world. Into which country, which family, which race or religion. Which, of course, is perhaps what they call fate? Which is, of course, utter nonsense? To suppose that some distant relative of a mythical God that we have never seen, never spoken with and who refuses to answer even the most ardent of prayers, is somehow the dictator of our destiny is the ramblings of a simpleton.’

‘To refuse, or to be unable to reveal himself may well be a blessing in disguise,' said the duchess. 'I'm sure if he did, there would be many people who would say that they were much better qualified to do the job. I cannot reveal him to you, Mr Chandler, but I can invite you to see his works, walking as we do in his footsteps and witnessing every scientific revelation of our age.’

‘Every invention we enjoy comes from the superior intellect in the mind of man,’ said Chandler with a degree of irritation.

‘But the materials we use for those inventions come from nature do they not? And we were gifted nature. Were we not? We did not create it.

But I grant you, without the hands of man it would fall into chaos. A chaos and atrophy not unlike a person's brain, who refuses to examine anything beyond his own opinions, content to wrestle with the weeds of the mind, don't you think Mr Chandler?'

‘I think perhaps the hands of man have already done irreparable damage,’ said Frau Bergmeier chuckling.

Chandler fell silent, somewhat at a loss as to what to say.

The duchess gave him her undivided attention and smiled at him as if every word that might fall from his lips were pearls to the needy.

He rose and bid them all goodnight.

'I find if you wish someone to stop talking, the best way is to listen to them! That way they hear the hollowness of their own words,' said the duchess finishing a large brandy.

A thought suddenly occurred to Frau Köehler and she decided to seize the opportunity of asking the duchess a question that all had wanted to know.

'Would you consider it impolite of me if I were to ask what the purpose of your visit to India is?' said Frau Köehler.

'Of course you may my dear! I'm surprised you haven't asked before.'

She sat back in her chair and told them the most fascinating story.

After the death of her husband, she had felt rather lost in life and without purpose. A very close friend of the family, a Mr Madge, a politician, was attempting to push a bill through parliament making it a criminal offence to entice young women to the East with the promise of a better life, but who finished up in the brothels of Bombay, in appalling conditions, serving the locals and sailors .In London she had created an organisation that helped fallen women.

Intriguingly, over the coming months, many women arrived back from Bombay with a letter from a gentleman there asking for her assistance. He had paid for their passage and enclosed funds to help them rehabilitate back into society.

The letters were almost illegible, leading her to believe that this man was either illiterate, which was unlikely as the letters were well crafted, or which, in all probability, that he had some disability which made writing difficult. She had never heard of such a generous and extraordinary man in her life and set about securing funds to travel to Bombay to meet him, hoping to enlist his help.

He never signed the letters, wishing to remain anonymous, and the women would not speak of him other than to say he was the kindest and bravest individual they had ever encountered.

The gentleman who handled his affairs in Bombay passed on his letters to her and was meeting the ship on her arrival, after which she would journey to Delhi to meet with the Viceroy and pass on correspondence from parliament that she was not at liberty to discuss.

'Sometimes,' she mused, 'despite the many evils in the world, there shines a spirit that leaves you breathless with admiration.'

~

The voyage had been uneventful so far. Only a brief stopover to shelter at Port Aden had been necessary, as the weather had become inclement but not alarming, which afforded time to restock much needed provisions and to take on fuel.

But on this quiet evening, when the ship was bathing in a warm ambience, the weather turned with a ferocity they had expected at The Cape.

So sudden did the wind change, that panic spread amongst the crew.

As the ship trimmed and crashed into the violent waves, there was consternation amongst the passengers.

Ushered in haste to their cabins, many were fearful that the ship was listing too much, watching tables and chairs sliding from port to starboard, fore and aft as the steamer rolled in the storm. The dark smoke rising from the funnels danced with the dark and heavy clouds, sending a deluge of rain, flooding the cabins, and turning the saloon into a rolling lake. No sooner had the water settled on the listing ship than it flowed in waves across the floor, disappearing through the draining slats that lined the skirting boards in the walls and seeped into steerage.

Crockery and cutlery were sent sprawling, and the Buxtons struggled to keep the finer china from falling from the ornate sideboards in the saloon: the carpets had been rolled up and placed well above the deck long before they had even approached The Cape.

~

As the passengers were confined to the cabin, the decks were all but deserted.

Chandler strapped his belt around the iron handrail and turned his face to the merciless waves that broke upon him.

'I love the ocean when she's angry!' he bellowed. 'Turbulent and unpredictable. Uncontrollable! How relentlessly she challenges our self-importance and makes us cling to every passing moment!'

He ranted and shouted above the storm like a man possessed.

'The future is always full of fear -so we believe! The fear of losing that tenuous grip we have on reality. Of parting with the acquisitions we treasure, the ideas we cling to, which become the measure of our pride!

In our quest for sanity that transcends the chaos of the human mind, our brothers in the east have always been much further down the path. Even in their poverty, we collect the crumbs at their feet, strewn like flora on the way, blown like spores from the garden of paradise; seeds that grow within the minds of men, and find a harvest in darker times, in tempests and storms when we lose our tether!'

He removed a flask from his coat and poured its contents down his throat, drinking in the water that beat against his face.

'I have mended these machines of flesh and blood, these countless chariots of bone that claw and gnaw relentlessly at life, insatiable in appetite. But still the mind plays havoc with man, torments itself, seeking its own destruction.

Like chiselled stone its divisions are carved and etched in our minds, and all the waters of the oceans cannot wash away the imprints of the past.

With each successive age we become more violent! Our understanding grows, marginally, but so does our sense of helplessness, bewilderment, and despair.

Having been given this extraordinary miracle of life, there are those who state that they are now the self-appointed gatekeepers at the womb and will dictate how you are to live your life! They will shape you in their own image, preparing you in every way to fit into a society they have created! Freedom is a messy business, it's true, and control is always appealing; unless, of course, you are the one being controlled. But the need of belonging, somewhere, anywhere, of identifying, is overwhelming and easily manipulated!

We are the fools of fortune! The legacy of dreams.'

~

Leaving his helmsman at the wheel, Captain Jarret strode calmly along the deck; a reassuring presence in times of panic. Many a time he had faced the perilous onslaught of the ocean.

He had seen the fear in men's eyes. The loss of hope in their hearts.

He'd watched as each man disappeared into the inner labyrinths of despair. How, faced with peril and possible death, morale plummets, and he fades into the infinite nothingness of his own mind where providence slips from your grasp like a drowning man and you confront the nakedness of your own spirit.

Water cascaded over the lower decks, and passengers in first class swore they could hear the screams of women and children in steerage. They had assumed they were the only ones on board, but the less desirable had been kept below deck and out of sight.

'Yes, I thought I'd find you here Chandler!' said the captain, shouting above the storm. 'You're a madman! You're going to catch your death!'

'Let it come! We must all face our demons Captain, they fall upon us day by day like sharp pointed arrows that pierce the fragile, superficial husks of men! Those shields and masks of delusional pride!

The human mind is still in its infancy.'

'You've been drinking Chandler. You should know better. Come on, pull yourself together man, you have responsibilities!'

He unstrapped his belt from the rail and helped him along the deck to the safety of his quarters.

'I love the ocean storms,' said Chandler, staggering below deck. 'The glory of her anger. The violence that cannot be controlled.'

Jarret rolled him into his bunk.

'The quest is futile, Jarret.'

'What quest be that Chandler?'

'The quest.... for the concord of man.'

He closed his eyes.

'The mind has become a market, Jarret, where we hoard and steal, barter and deceive. We are merely buyers and sellers now of goods and dreams in this sordid and torrid existence.'

'It's how we survive Chandler. There isn't a creature or plant on earth that exists except by consuming or destroying another.'

Chandler had already drifted off into a drunken stupor.

~

That night, the storm passed and the ship sailed on in calmer seas.

The captain knew the oceans well and was no stranger to her sudden whims. As a younger man, he had learned to trust the old windjammers before steam had swept aside the wooden sailing ships. When iron made the Empire wealthier.

He had learned to hand, steer, and reef the sails, keeping the watch on freezing nights, shivering, alone with the stars.

On winter mornings he had seen sailors leave their fingers on the handrails. Ripped from their hands by the bitter ice.

Sail was free, and now the fuel was more expensive, but the voyages were quicker than before when he had brought the jute and rice from India, and the wool from Australia.

A greater skill was needed to sail the wooden ships, and he missed them. His cabin walls were draped with pictures of vessels from another time. Ghosts that are now laid buried in a watery grave; a thousand souls that had braved the waves, now whispering from the ocean's deep.

~

The next morning, Captain Jarret knocked at Chandler's cabin - there was no response. He opened the door quietly to find him out cold, still recovering from the after-effects of his drinking bout. Chandler didn't drink often.

Jarret had sailed on many a voyage with him and he was as hard as a rock, but every man has his demons.

Often when the tempests struck, and the ocean was plunged into darkness, would he find him on deck in a state of delirium. Raging at the storm, as if deep beneath that self-disciplined veneer raged a tormented spirit, harnessed and suppressed.

In all the time he had known him, Chandler had never talked about his past. Never confided his hidden torments. He was the finest doctor he had sailed with, but he had never got to know the man. As if he had built a shield of steel around himself, impenetrable. And his gruff and rude exterior was a warning not to pry.

He had saved many who had been near to death and tended them with ruthless care, as if losing them was an admission of failure for which he would carry the burden, the chains of guilt. The standards he set himself he expected from others and was unsympathetic to weakness. But illness was different. It was invidious. Seemingly illogical. He was fighting another enemy, hidden and tenacious beneath the flesh and buried in the mind.

On the rare occasions when Chandler had to amputate a diseased limb, Jarret would often watch him work. He was mesmerised by the way he watched his hands working, rather than the instruments and the flesh beneath. It was as if all the knowledge he needed was there at his fingertips, where the working surfaces met and he was just a passive observer.

Medicine had for a long time passed from the realm of magic to science, but it seemed as if he was letting his hands instruct him, as if he was being guided by an unseen force.

Afterwards they would often sit together in silence, lost in a kind of melancholy, when the shadows in the corner would visit, and the sound of the waves like predators would hypnotise them in a kind of darkness when consciousness was suspended. Not the welcome release of sleep they shared with every living being, but a silent invitation, an outstretched hand from the shadows to open doors, forbidden or slammed shut by fear and the absence of light - when shadows play havoc with the mind.

Few had sensed the coming storm when it had arrived, but Captain Jarret had seen the warning signs: the low dark clouds, the rising of the winds and the drop in temperature. The flashes on the horizon had told him it was only hours away and he calmly told the crew to prepare the ship, but even he hadn't anticipated just how quickly the weather would turn.

When it struck, two areas of low pressure had created an upward draught and so the storm had split, circling the ship like a tropical dance, tossing it like a cork in a bath.

He had seen it often as a young sailor returning from Java on the galleons off the coasts of Sumatra, the squalls and thunderstorms in the Straits of Malacca, the monsoon surges, and violent winds.

But nothing was feared more than diseases. Typhoid, typhus from lice and chiggers, and venereal diseases caught at Port.

Rats were a serious problem, and constant inspections ensured the colonies didn't establish themselves below deck .A mischief, and sometimes a hundred or more in a pack, but Jarret made the crew arrange regular checks, to look for droppings, gnawing of ropes and grease. Copious layers of Paris Green were painted in the nooks and crannies of the ship, in the dark and hidden places fiercely protected by the rodents, which made the lower decks smell of garlic, and later was found to be toxic and deadly. Not only could it deter rats but could also kill people; they found that arsenic grew in mould painted with the substance.

Jarret walked the decks checking on any damage, securing the lifeboats, checking the rigging.

He looked up at the masts creaking in the wind.

As a boy he had loved that sound. It rekindled the romantic naivety of youth.

The stretching and cracking of the wood, the waves lapping at the hull. The treenails groaning as if they would split in the gentle winds .As if a thousand trees, once tall and root-strong, now buoyant, float with tar and tallow, and sensually part the warm erotic waves, caressing the ocean's skin with bows of lumber. Her heave and sway, her surge and roll, her pitch and yaw, tumbling, enfolded in her lover's arms.

Youth has a way with honeyed words that often fade with the ravages of time. They make us smile and leave an affectionate memory of what we thought our lives would be.

And now the plating of the steel hull, flexing like an oil drum, brittle, strident, cut the ocean like a knife and made her bleed.

The sails were wrapped away to stop the rats eating them, but they were still supposed to use them to sail into harbour to save on expense.

That was one of his favourite parts of the voyage. When the sails were luffing, he could feel the ship come alive again. Breathing. Sucking in the wind. Whistling through the halyards. One day, the sails and the masts would all but disappear, he thought, as steam becomes more reliable. Having the masts now was really more about weight and balance than as a back-up, although the forward mast was still useful as a crane for loading cargo at the ports.

He thought these new ships had abandoned the wind, cast her aside, groaning as if in perpetual pain - betrayed. In revenge, they sent storms and tempests, as they sliced their way through the torrents like an iron dragon belching black smoke, polluting the air and choking the lungs.

The sounds that fill the air and assault the ears, in this new age of grease and grime, of soot and sin were a clamour of strident discord. The brittle clash of iron and steel had seemed as if the dark arts had risen, manifested, and robbed them of their silence. It was a quieter world when he was young.

It'll all end in tears, he thought. *For money drives the future now. Profit, greed and gain.*

On the whole sailors are philosophical souls and live much nearer to nature, are more respectful of her power. They learn her ways, submit, and are emboldened by her challenges; humbled by the ocean's unknowable empty silences, her violent rage.

More sea than land this earth that she has cracked and fractured into islands and nations. For those who have traversed her waves, absorbed her mysteries, they carry the ocean forever in their minds.

~

Chandler stood in his cabin looking at himself in the mirror; for a long time, he stood. Just staring.

The reflection seemed to speak to him.

'So, there ya are my boy! Looking like me now, aren't ya? Told you ya would, didn't I? Not so smug now, eh? Not so easy openin' doors, is it? Easier to slam 'em in your face.

That's what life'll do to ya son. You'll see. Gotta grow a thicker skin. Weather the storm. You stay out there in the cold 'till the thunderstorm passes. It'll do ya good. Toughen ya up. Ya can come in when she's gone. It's only a storm. It's only a storm, son - stop snivelling!'

Young Chandler sat on the damp concrete floor by the outside toilet. He would have sheltered there, but the flies, spider webs, and smell of urine made him feel ill.

With his back against the grimy black bricks of the wall, he tried to sleep, but the thunder resounded down the alleyway, the gale rattling the latch and blowing the wooden door of the yard open, as it crashed against the broken fence and rocked the stolen railway sleepers, still black with tar.

Lightning lit up the yard and rubbish bins rolled down the lane, smashing into garden walls and scattering their contents, which spiralled up in the wind, up over the tenements and chimney pots of the city of grime.

He hugged his knees to his chest as the rain saturated his clothes and drenched his hair. The sound was deafening.

He looked up at the bedroom window to see the curtains being drawn.

It was dark by the time the woman left.

'Go on, luv,' she said. 'You can go in now .He's drunk and fast asleep.'

She gave him some money and kissed him on his cheek, the smell of alcohol lingered on her breath, like all the others. He listened to the sound of her shoes echoing down the alleyway, as her cheap perfume faded in the rain.

His father died that night. His final breath was the beginning of a life abandoned. His mother had left years before.

He was taken to the city orphanage where the nuns were brutal, cruel, sadistic. The children worked mercilessly for everything they got, which wasn't much.

In the darkness of their dormitories, cold and damp, where the wind whistled through the cracks like an old man's teeth, the children used to whisper that God must have given up on that place.

So had he.

In desperation, one evening he climbed through the window and ran away, hiding in the eerie quietness of a cleaning cupboard at the local Hospital.

Squalor and infection were rife with little clean water and no air. Their nicknames as 'The Houses of Death' were well given, but somehow he'd thrived.

One evening he was found by a friendly nurse who gave him food and helped him find work on the wards. From her he had learned to read and write, and she offered him a room in her attic. She gave him the only real comfort and affection he had ever known. Surrounded by medical journals, he immersed himself in her world.

There was no formal training for physicians and surgeons. They were given an apprenticeship if they were lucky and learned on the job. They read about the medicines, the instruments, and learned the art of cutting.

He would often see bits of flesh stuck to their aprons, and blood on the floors, hearing the muffled screams echoing in the long corridors, and the faint smell of chloroform and iodine permeated the wards.

The nurse's kindness wove a tapestry of trust and closeness in him, but she had attracted the attention of an older surgeon, and caught in a delicate flattery and admiration, she hadn't realised that beneath the veneer of gallant compliments, the surgeon's intentions were not as pure as she had thought.

He was married, with children, and she had become pregnant. In a desperate attempt to cover his shame, she and the child had died during the operation.

She was only in her twentieth year - a child herself.

With all-consuming rage, Chandler smashed the mirror on the cabin wall with his fist. Shards cascaded to the floor, a symbol of the shattered remnants of his past.

He swept them aside with his foot and fell into his bunk, drifting off into delirium.

Within days, he had resumed his duties, and the shadows of his memories descended into the hidden dark and intricate labyrinths of despair.

~

Jarret had noticed the change that had come over the passengers and crew since the storm had subsided.

He knew all too well the power of the ocean. Its effect on the mind. How it challenges your sanity.

In the tumultuous tempests of the open seas, the human spirit, like a frail vessel tossed upon capricious waves, undergoes a profound metamorphosis. The howling winds, laden with the salted breath of Poseidon, whip through the sails of the ship, their mournful wails echoing the inner tumult of those who dare to traverse the tempestuous seas.

Amidst the chaos and conflicting emotions, fear, that primeval instinct, coils around the heart like a serpent, injecting its venom of doubt and trepidation. Each thunderous crash of the waves against the hull reverberates within the soul and plucks at the delicate heart strings of human vulnerability.

Yet, paradoxically, there exists within this maelstrom, a perverse exhilaration; an intoxicating cocktail of adrenaline and awe. The flickering lightning illuminates faces contorted by the shadows, revealing expressions that oscillate between terror and a strange ecstasy. The very elements conspire to awaken dormant instincts, to remind the mariner of their fragile existence in the grand theatre of nature.

As the ship is tossed upon violent seas, a battle ensues within the minds of men, the relentless onslaught of wind and wave creates internal tempests, as the crew grapple with the demons of doubt and the spectre of mortality.

Every creak and groan of the ship's timber echoes with impending disaster. In the aftermath of such a nautical ordeal, survivors emerge changed, marked by the indelible scars of their mental odyssey. The storm at sea, with its elemental fury, serves not only as a crucible of fear but as an alchemist's cauldron, transmuting the base metal of human frailty into the tempered steel of resilience and courage. For those who weather the storm, who bear the scars of fear and awe, an indomitable spirit is birthed from the maelstrom of adversity.

12. RUDGWICK'S DISTRESS.

A sombre darkness filled Rudgwick's dimly lit cabin as he slept. Beyond the flickering flame of the lamp, his thoughts, like a ship navigating uncharted waters, sailed toward the distant shores of India.

The very mention of this exotic land had stirred such curiosity within him. The allure of the East, with its mystic spices, vibrant silks, and tales of ancient wisdom intrigued his young mind and inflamed his imagination. For a young man who had rarely ventured beyond the confines of London, it felt like a baptism of fire.

He envisioned the bustling bazaars, where merchants traded in gold, and fragrant teas wafted through the air like whispers of a distant siren, and the grandeur of exotic architecture, standing resolute against the passage of time, sparkled vividly in his mind.

And yet, amidst this enchanting imagery, a solemn reflection cast its shadow. Although he had not firsthand experience, from what he had read, the jewel in the imperial crown, India, bore witness to an intricate conflict of cultures, prosperity and hardship. He grappled with the dichotomy of a land steeped in opulence, and the weight of its colonial past and present.

As he traced the contours of maps and devoured accounts of far-off lands, an inescapable truth dawned upon him—the East held within its heart hidden stories, untold and histories complex.

For India was not merely a tableau of exotic wonders, but a living, breathing entity with its own struggles and triumphs.

In the quiet solitude of his cabin, Rudgwick found himself at a crossroads of fascination and contemplation.

The allure of India, wrapped in the folds of time, beckoned him as a novice explorer of the art of travel, but even more the uncharted territories within his own mind.

In the bustling thoroughfares of Bombay, he dreamed of navigating the intricacies of colonial India, finding himself ensnared in its mesmerising flames. Amidst the clamour of street vendors hawking their wares and the vibrant hues of traditional saris, he had chanced upon the captivating Frau Bergmeier. A German beauty transplanted to the Indian soil, who possessed an ethereal grace that set her apart from the kaleidoscope of native women. Her porcelain complexion glowed softly under the Indian sun, and her turquoise eyes sparkled with an untamed spirit. Clad in a flowing gown that mirrored the vibrant glow of the East, she moved with a measured elegance that left Rudgwick momentarily breathless.

Their serendipitous encounter unfolded amidst the mingling scents of spices and the distant strains of indigenous melodies. He, a blend of curiosity and chivalry, removed his hat and engaged in polite discourse with the beguiling German Frau. Their exchange, punctuated by the polite cadence of Victorian manners bore witness to the collision of worlds converging in the heat of a bustling Indian city.

As they conversed, he glimpsed the intricacies of her world. Her tales painted vivid portraits of tea parties under the Indian sky and soirées where German propriety met the exuberance of Indian festivities. A symbiotic fusion of cultures unfolded before him, and in her company he found himself enchanted by the harmonious coexistence of disparate lands.

In that fleeting moment, amidst the vibrant tableau of colonial India, the destinies of Mr. Rudgwick and Frau Bergmeier collided. Their encounter, a fleeting chapter in the grand narrative of the subcontinent, resonated with the echoes of an era where the threads of fate wove tales as diverse and captivating as the land itself.

And as it sometimes is with dreams, a veil was dropped, a chiffon cloud that gently swept the scene aside, and he found himself amidst the splendour of a colonial ball, where flickering gas lamps cast an ephemeral glow upon the polished parquet, and once again he caught sight of the resplendent Frau Bergmeier - a vision that had stirred the depths of his innocence.

Frau Bergmeier, a paragon of Teutonic beauty and sophistication, eclipsed the room with her poise and grace. Clad in an exquisite gown that mirrored the opulence of her surroundings, she bore the regality of a Maharani amidst the swirling tapestry of dancers. Rudgwick, a novice in the labyrinth of social intricacies, felt a palpable tremor as he became obsessed with her radiance.

In the quixotic dance of the ballroom, like a moth drawn to the flame, he found himself ensnared by her allure. Her turquoise eyes, pools of wisdom that belied her youth, held knowledge of diverse experiences that were for him unknown.

He had discovered an intellect that far surpassed his own, each exchange leaving him acutely aware of his vast innocence of the ways of the world. Mesmerised, he slowly took her in his arms. Her lips both soft and sensual. Her mouth, inviting. Slowly and gently, he felt her slender body as his hands... his hands...

Rudgwick awoke and turned over in his bunk. His clothes and sheets were saturated with perspiration and his pulse was racing at an alarming rate. Shocked, he clambered over to the basin and splashed his face with cold water. The vividness of his dream made him embarrassed by its contents. A sordid mixture of Penny Dreadfuls and cheap romantic tales of suppressed lust. His innocent youth had removed a veil that covered the deep suppressed erotic desires he had denied, controlled, and made him tremble that when he next looked into Frau Bergmeier's eyes, his passion would betray him.

13. LONDON. CHANCERY LANE.

There is a certain comfort to be drawn from the familiar, thought Sir Ranulph, as his carriage turned into Chancery Lane through the morning fog that clung to the city walls with desperate fingers of grime and filth.

The certainties of life, especially when one has passed the age of frivolity, offer at least a certain structure when the mind is not as agile as once it was.

In the bustling streets of London, amidst the cabs and carriages and the ceaseless flow of humanity, there exists a peculiar solace in the predictable. The comforting sound of well-worn cobblestones underfoot, the timeworn facades of familiar shops, the hollow, dull and foreboding sound of the church bell, and the enduring presence of the old lamp post at the corner – these are the anchors that tether the weary soul in the turbulent sea of urban existence.

In the labyrinthine alleys, where darkness whispers of bygone tales of alarum and gruesome undertakings in the shadows of depravity, one finds sanctuary in the predictability of the known. For in the midst of life's tumult, it is the thread of familiarity that gives us reassurance; a testament to the enduring charm of the tried and tested amidst the ever-changing panorama of the city of London.

Amidst the swirling fog that clung to the sticky, black, and damp cobblestones of Chancery Lane, Sir Ranulph found his carriage enveloped in an alarming spectacle.

A dishevelled figure, clad in tattered rags, emerged from the shadows; her countenance bearing the weight of desolation, the trappings of poverty and the stench of a harlot's room.

With a fevered gaze, the wretched soul extended a trembling hand, revealing fingers stained with the indelible marks of hardship.

As the carriage trundled forward, the forlorn creature implored him with a broken voice. The passersby averted their eyes, unwilling to confront the stark reality etched upon the visage of destitution. Sir Ranulph, ever the compassionate warrior of human suffering, felt the pangs of empathy surge within him. For in that fleeting moment, the bustling thoroughfare of Chancery Lane became a stage where the drama of societal neglect unfolded in all its poignant tragedy.

Sir Ranulph removed his purse to offer the unfortunate creature some little coinage when several dark unkempt and dishevelled men leapt into the carriage and grabbed his purse, striking him hard upon the chin before disappearing into the darkened alleyways that led away from the common thoroughfare, and into the web of lanes that coiled down the crumbling steps to the hidden rat's nests of poverty and destitution.

Pulling the carriage to a halt and calming the horses, the driver opened the flap and asked if he was in need of assistance and whether he should summon a police constable, but Sir Ranulph was of a hardy disposition and not so easily upset by misfortune. He assured him he all was well but asked him to return to his club where he could replenish his purse.

So far, the day had not proven to be the comfort of familiarity he had hoped; although, both crime and skulduggery was, and no doubt always would be, a familiar occurrence.

As a young man in his dimly lit chambers, where the flickering candlelight had cast a shadow upon volumes of legal tomes, he had pondered the wretched tales of destitution and misfortune within the hallowed halls of justice. Through the clouded and murky lens of the law, he had beheld the impoverished souls, clad in tattered garments, their eyes reflecting the bitterness of life's cruel caprice.

With each case, he had navigated the intricate tales of human suffering, piecing together the fragments of desperation and despair. The courtroom, a stage for the unfolding drama of wretched lives, often echoed with the laments of those whose dreams had crumbled like ancient ruins.

As a barrister, a stoic figure, he had found himself a reluctant witness to this societal discord. In the hallowed silence of legal deliberation, he had dissected the narratives of broken families, penury-stricken urchins, and the forsaken, all seeking solace beneath the blindfolded Lady of Justice.

With ink-stained quill, he had etched the legal remedies upon parchment, yet the ink seemed but feeble balm for the festering wounds and bitterness of misfortune.

Sir Ranulph's heart, though encased in the stern facade of legal decorum, could not entirely escape the tendrils of empathy that wrapped around the souls laid bare before him.

In those quiet hours of reflection, he had grappled with the paradox of a system designed to mete out justice, yet often swayed by the capricious winds of society's indifference.

And at the end of day, when the meagre fire had burnt out and the final cracks of light had crept along the narrow lane like a weary traveller seeking rest, he had laid down his quill, closed his legal volumes, and carried the weight of the unfortunate in his thoughts.

A sombre reminder that within the grand edifice of the law, there existed chambers where the echoes of misfortune resounded with haunting persistence.

Later that afternoon, Sir Ranulph returned to his chambers to collect the mail. The old lock on the office door still stubbornly resisting, but eventually relenting, as it always did.

In the dimly lit corridor, a missive had arrived from the far reaches of Bombay, bearing the weighty words of Doctor Surinda. The quill scratched across the parchment, unravelling a tale of intrigue that would send shivers through the legal corridors of India. The barrister's eyes, weary from years of scrutinising legal tomes, widened with a mixture of astonishment and disbelief.

The revered Colonel Faulkner, once thought to have succumbed to the shadows of his own despair, was, in fact, a victim of foul play.

Murder, most foul whispered the ink-stained pages, as the barrister's mind raced to unravel the intricate web woven by sinister hands.

The candle flickered ominously as he delved into the details, his ageing fingers tracing the contours of each damning revelation. A tale of deceit unfolded before him, and the spectre of evil loomed large.

Sir Ranulph, with newfound vigour, vowed to expose the malevolence pulling the strings from the shadows of betrayal. He determined to embark on a quest for truth, propelled by a sense of duty that transcended the confines of his seasoned profession.

The echoes of intrigue resonated in the air as he became an unwitting protagonist in a tale where injustice, like a beacon in the fog, beckoned from the distant shores of India.

He assumed that as Rudgwick would soon arrive in Bombay, he would be better informed of the entire developments, and decided to wait and take advice for what his younger partner considered to be the best way to precede in this unfortunate situation. Setting quill to parchment, he nonetheless wrote his own opinion of the best course to take while the matter was fresh in his mind, but refrained from posting it until he had received word from Rudgwick, and would have a clearer picture of events as they had unfolded.

With a heavy heart he returned to his club In St James's, seeking comfort in the crystal decanters of fine wine and the contemplative balm and quiet contemplation of a large cigar, anxiously awaiting news from his young partner.

14. APPROACHING THE GATE OF INDIA.

The pilot from the tugboat that was to pull the ship into the colonial port of Bombay, arrived at dawn. He was greeted by the captain and together they discussed their approach, which had to be done with the utmost care, as many ships had already docked, and several lay at sea awaiting their allotted time or clearance of their demurrage, before approaching the harbour and unloading their cargoes of goods and passengers who had sailed from every corner of the globe.

After the tugs had secured their ropes, a ceremonial salute, which sent jets of coloured water into the air, welcomed the ship as it pulled it around the sandbanks in the approaching estuary.

Even at this distance, from the port the smell of exotic spices carried on the breeze permeated the ship and a deluge of sea birds hung above the masts waiting anxiously and impatiently for a much-anticipated early feed.

Many a lady had been terrified by swooping birds attacking the artificial fruit and flowers in their hats, snatching them from their heads and flying off, much to the amusement of the passengers in steerage. One unfortunate woman ran along the deck, frantically flapping her arms and looking as if she was attempting flight, and screaming like a hockey girl, only to be unceremoniously sent sprawling with her dress above her head, revealing petticoats and pantaloons and a much-distressed husband in pursuit.

After a strong dose of smelling salts, she was accompanied to her cabin, weeping uncontrollably and beating her irate husband with a barrage of blows with what was left of her parasol.

~

Rudgwick seized a last opportunity to walk with Frau Bergmeier before they disembarked. There was a sadness in her face, and he sensed she was still burdened with feelings she had not resolved.

'Forgive me asking but...did he hurt you very much, Frau Bergmeier?'

She didn't look at him but sighed. It was a long time since she had allowed herself to retrace her past.

'He was an incurable alcoholic... I...was very young, Mr Rudgwick. Very...naive. And I quite fell to pieces emotionally. He would not allow me out alone and would lock me in the room. He said if I ever left him, he would kill himself. He was violent and would drag me by the hair and often assault me.

Then he would cry and say how sorry he was and how much he loved me, and I forgave him, but the bruises were hard to conceal.'

Rudgwick looked at her in disbelief, bewildered that anyone should have experienced such appalling things at such a young age, and realised in that moment what a sheltered, uncomplicated life he'd had, and how fortunate he had been.

'I am so sorry, Frau Bergmeier.'

'Frau Köehler helped me escape one evening when he was the worse for drink. 'She paused, struggling with what to say next and trying to choose her words carefully. 'He... killed himself, Mr Rudgwick. He put his head in a gas oven.'

They were both silent for a long while. He looked at her as the morning sun shone on her face and filled the strands of her hair with dancing light.

She stood staring at the approaching harbour, which seemed so vibrant in colour, compared to the feelings of despair within her.

'I blame myself.'

'No, please do not! He was obviously ill and irrational. You cannot manipulate or control someone. That cannot be love.'

'Love is a waywood horse Mr Rudgwick. One never knows where it will lead you. I was changed. He was a brilliant pianist. I believed, in my innocence, that I could cure him of his dependency. But some people you cannot help. They give you too heavy a burden to share.'

Rudgwick looked at her with sadness and deep affection.

It had been a long time since someone had looked at her that way.

She kissed him gently on his cheek and took his arm as the ship's horn signalled their arrival at the port of Bombay.

15. BOMBAY.

As the ship cut through the waters, the air thickened with the scent of spices and vibrant hues of a bustling Indian port city. A melange of aromas: cinnamon, cardamom, and exotic perfumes wafted through the sea breeze and painted a vivid sensory tapestry.

A heaving mass of humanity crowded the port, begging for food and what work they could get. They docked, but before the ropes were even secured, they swarmed up the sides of the ship. Shouting, offering help.

The crew were merciless in beating them back with sticks, and many fell into the estuary or cowered on the deck clutching desperately to whatever they could.

As the group arrived on deck, they looked on in horror. Never had they witnessed such poverty and hunger or desperation. Not even in the hidden streets of London, where disease and death were a daily ritual politely kept from delicate eyes.

Chandler shouted at the crew to stop, forcibly hitting the sailors and throwing them off and placing himself between them.

He was a tall and powerful man, and the crew were reluctant to challenge him. 'Chandler Sahib! Chandler Sahib! Need help, Sahib!!'

'I will come to the clinic later and do what I can! You must leave now. I will come!!'

They clambered down the ropes, but not before kissing his hands and his feet many times. Dignity and self-respect will not feed your children here. That was for another world.

The scene before them made the group stagger in disbelief.

'Someone dies every two hours here,' said Chandler.

'Malnutrition, Cholera, Polio, Gonorrhoea. Welcome to India, Madam. Where is your God, now?'

The duchess stood, shaking with anger at the treatment of these helpless souls. Frau Bergmeier had tears in her eyes, while Rudgwick tried to maintain as much control as he could muster and comforted Frau Köehler, who appeared as if she would faint and to be near to vomiting, clutching a handkerchief to her mouth which smelled of rose water. The flies distressed her as they buzzed around the hold where food was being unloaded.

The shock of such disorganised chaos spread fear amongst the passengers. The ones in steerage were not so moved, being of a hardier constitution. They were used to suffering, but several had not survived the voyage and would be carried off the ship when everyone had disembarked, and night had fallen.

Eventually the port authority sent officers to control the crowd and pushed them back behind wooden barriers so that the passengers could leave the ship.

As they slowly walked down the gangplank, they looked back at hundreds of faces peering through the lower potholes. Some terrified, some smiling despite everything; hungry and unwashed.

Was this the same ship they had travelled on for many months? Never in their wildest dreams had they suspected that in the decks below, such misery and deprivation lurked - a living hell.

How isolated they had been from other people's suffering.

In their sudden shame they walked with heads bowed to the waiting carriage, not daring to look into the desperate, pleading eyes of want. Here, death was never far away.

The group sat in silence as they were driven in the carriage over the cracked uneven cobblestones of the old harbour, each trying to process the chaos they had all witnessed.

They looked out at the ships at anchor, waiting to dock and be unloaded, and those stretched along the harbour wall, their gunny sacks breathing in the stagnant air lay stacked on the jetty or being loaded onto oxen carts for the warehouses, the markets, and mountain villages.

There was sullenness or sombre insolence in the faces of the workers who kept their eyes lowered in subservience as the carriage trundled passed. Women on the crowded pavements stopped and stared at the clothes they were wearing, while their saris, a kaleidoscope of bright vibrant colours, seemed to sparkle in the late morning sun. Turquoise and yellow, blue and red.

In contrast to the bright and joyous colours, the beggars in little less than a loin cloth and without legs, pushed themselves along on wooden boards, and the blind lingered on every corner shaking a metal tin that rattled with small coins, waking the vagrants that slept along the railway lines, who threw stones at them as they stumbled into dark alleyways chased by stray dogs.

They were overwhelmed by a current of sensual emotion, both dangerous and alarming. A whirlwind of chaos almost unbearable in its febrile intensity, when your senses are brought to a threshold of delirium, and all control seems as if it will vanish, boil over, in a maelstrom of pain and anguish.

The duchess looked with fresh eyes and apprehension into the eyes of hordes of desperate people almost crawling over each other to survive.

If this is the fruit of Empire, she thought, it smells sweet in decay.

And would the glory of the British Raj bring hidden shame, to dull the glint of this our finest jewel.

~

As they made their way through Kala Ghoda Art District, they came upon an iron structure that appeared to grow from the earth like a huge skeletal birdcage. The duchess recognised it from sketches she had seen in the newspapers in England.

'Ah!' she exclaimed, 'at least on my return I can inform Mr Watson that his hotel project comes on apace.

We seem to be entering another iron age. Although it sometimes feels as if we never left it. It's everywhere in all its ugliness. Buildings, ships, and weapons. Machines that sound like the hammers of Hell!

It's strange how the last one also ended with an invasion. I sincerely hope that the British Raj will be as beneficial to the

Colonies as the Romans were for us. But somehow, I have my doubts.

Perhaps, on reflection, I am being a little unkind and my judgement premature.

In England I was fortunate to be shown a work in progress by a family friend - the sculptor, Adrian Jones. Do you know him?

His work was entitled “'Peace and the Quadriga descending from Heaven.”

I distinctly remember his benefactor, Lord Michelham's son, being somewhat sullen as he stood being sculpted.

Although standing for hours holding a set of reins tied to a chair whilst completely naked was probably not his idea of a jovial afternoon. We were quite shocked, I recall, but artists have never been respectful of others' sensibilities. The armature of the sculpture was enormous, and I had my doubts that he would ever finish it. Maybe one day. Who knows, perhaps this skeletal monstrosity of a hotel, this naked armature of iron, when finished will also bring peace to this troubled land. I hope so, but... time will tell, as it tells all.'

The carriage came to a halt outside a charmingly quaint hotel, and they were pleasantly surprised to find that they all had reservations for the same residence.

Frau Köehler had not spoken since leaving the ship and had originally been agitated that her dearest friend had chosen such an unappealing city for their sabbatical. But, as it was a gift from her, she did not feel justified in complaining and bore it with worthy stoicism, trying to rid her mind of the horrific scenes she had just witnessed. But the opulence of the hotel went a considerable way to easing her concerns.

Here, in the heart of bustling Bombay, amidst the rickshaws and the vibrancy of cultural life, they entered a venerable colonial hotel, its facade adorned with intricate carvings that whispered tales of a bygone era.

As the group entered the hotel reception, a vestibule of grandeur greeted them with polished mahogany furniture and a Persian carpet that bore witness to decades of footsteps. Walls adorned with fading portraits and aged maps would speak in ages yet to come of an era when the British Empire left an indelible mark on the Indian subcontinent.

As they stepped across the threshold, the echoes of history reverberated through the air, the architecture mirroring the intersection of old-world charm and the dawn of a new culture. The ornate pillars and arches, reminiscent of colonial opulence, stood in stark contrast to the vibrant hues of Indian fabrics that adorned the surroundings, weaving a visual symphony that encapsulated the fusion of two worlds.

The reception desk, an antique mahogany monolith, bore the marks of time, its surface etched with the stories of countless travellers who sought refuge within its shadow. The quill pens and inkwells hinted at an era when handwritten ledgers chronicled the comings and goings of esteemed guests.

The group stood with wide-eyed admiration beaming with delight.

Beyond the hotel's confines, the bustling harbour infused the air with a medley of scents that wafted through the open windows. The heady aroma of exotic spices mingled with the salty breath of the Arabian Sea, a testament to the convergence of trade and tradition. As goods were unloaded from ships, the symphony of clinking crates and the distant calls of merchants created a canvas that painted the vibrant pulse of Bombay's burgeoning identity.

In this colonial oasis, the reception of the old hotel stood as a silent witness between tradition and transition, a testament to the ever-evolving tapestry of life.

'I wish I could take credit for choosing this hotel, but it was arranged for me,' said Frau Bergmeier.

'As was mine,' said Rudgwick.

'It appears you were all lucky enough to choose the same agent,' suggested the duchess, 'but my suite was kindly arranged by the gentleman I told you of.'

She removed the letter from her purse. 'A... Doctor Surinda.'

'Doctor Surinda!?'exclaimed Rudgwick.

'Doctor Surinda!?' said Frau Bergmeier, 'but... that is also the gentleman I shall be meeting.'

'And I!' said Rudgwick.

They all looked at each other in astonishment and with mouths wide open.

'Well,' said the duchess, 'this is most surprising and mysterious. It would appear that fate has thrown us together, and we remain joined at the hip for the foreseeable future.

How intriguing. How exciting!'

They all agreed that after they had changed and rested, they would meet that evening in the hotel lounge at eight of the clock, when Doctor Surinda would arrive and no doubt a suitable explanation would be found, and all would be revealed.

Rudgwick, distracted by the opulence of his surroundings, lingered by the walls of books which stretched magnificently from floor to ceiling.

The hotel manager walked down the marble staircase and stood behind him.

'Many of these are gifts left by previous visitors. Some by the original authors themselves who enjoyed the quiet ambience of our hotel.

This one,' he said, pulling out a leather-bound volume well-travelled and worn at the edges, 'was given to the hotel a long time ago, before I came, by a young Rudyard Kipling I believe.

To my shame I am not an avid reader, but I believe she has achieved some degree of notoriety already.'

Rudgwick smiled, and politely refrained from correcting him.

The hotel manager was a very jovial rotund gentleman who seemed to take his responsibilities extremely seriously. His meticulous eye for detail ensured that standards of the highest quality were maintained, and the hotel exuded the charm and impressiveness one would expect, and that no doubt it was famous for.

As the luggage was slowly and carefully unloaded from the carriage and taken to their rooms the hotel manager inquired with genuine curiosity.

'How does England compare to our beloved Bombay, Mr Rudgwick? I have never been fortunate enough to have visited your country. Of course one hears stories, but nothing compares to a first-hand account from someone who is from the illustrious seat of Empire.'

For a moment Rudgwick found it difficult to transplant himself back into the country he had left, as he had experienced so many things already on his voyage.

'In England,' explained Rudgwick, 'the landscapes in Spring and Summer are covered with lush greenery; in Autumn, it is as if the gardens have been bathed in burnished gold; and in Winter, it is covered in a delicate blanket of snow which no matter how regal or squalid the abode, lends everything a charming and magical equality. It is truly the most wonderful time of year- for those who are fortunate enough to be able to afford to indulge in the magnificent wares displayed in the shop windows.

It is a delight to watch the gas lamps flicker on the presents and gifts, the beautiful sweets and lush winter bouquets of holly and pinecones and red berries adorning the shop facades. The scent of which is intoxicating.

The music-boxes and marionettes hanging from the drooping branches of pine trees are barely visible through the frosted glass and steamed-up dimpled windows dripping with condensation.

The sounds of carriage wheels are gently muffled by the straw strewn on the road, and children wrapped up warm in coats and mufflers push their cold noses against baker's windows steaming with sweetmeats and pies, egg-glazed and brown-crusted in the windows of darkened alleyways that once had caused a passing concern by wary people but now shone with the magic of a season that warmed all hearts both rich and poor, who for the briefest of time are transported from the dark and grey and sombre streets by the smiles and greetings from a populace grateful to be alive in this time of diseases as they follow the church bell to the altar of our Lord to give thanks for the blessings of life amidst the darkness of the city.'

Rudgwick found himself becoming somewhat melancholy about London as he remembered the warm ambience of cold winter evenings, the smell of coal dust and the sweet scent of wood-ash.

'But in stark contrast to the vibrant hues of Bombay, the cold of England is often merciless and unforgiving. The architecture is regal and elegant, mostly cold but sometimes quaint and deceptively charming in its decay.

While here, every corner is ablaze with colour.

Every face seems to glow with the miracle of life, the sheer joy of a shared wonder they have been blessed with. The heat of the sun and the abundance of nature that seems to laugh as it tumbles over itself, gently searching for a portion of the blinding light to nourish a cacophony of colour, an intoxication of flora and fauna, scents and smells, and the tastes of paradise.'

The manager beamed with delight as Rudgwick continued. Walking to the window, he stared out at the bustling streets and vibrancy of life.

'There is an undeniable vitality, a pulse that resonates through its crowded streets,' said Rudgwick. 'The diversity of cultures, languages, and traditions creates a mosaic of life that I have never experienced.

England, for all its sophistication, might lack the kaleidoscope of diversity that Bombay so effortlessly weaves together.'

The hotel manager opened the window and a gentle wave of air wafted across the reception hall, momentarily warming the cool breeze that came from the ceiling fans.

'Each city has its own heartbeat, it is true, a rhythm that defines its essence. Bombay, with its contradictions and harmonies, stands as a beauty of diversity, vibrancy and resilience. A rich interplay of contrasts.

But like most cities there are areas one should avoid, Mr Rudgwick. I do not believe, if one is cautious, that you would be in danger, but those places are frighteningly overcrowded and dilapidated and it could be overwhelming for those who might wander from the main thoroughfare and who may inadvertently stumble into them. Please keep me informed of your itinerary and I will be happy to advise you and arrange suitable escorts.'

'As I am here on business, I suspect there may be little time for sightseeing, but we shall see.'

The hotel manager smiled.

'India has a way of changing people, Mr Rudgwick. Even those who demand her conformity. She has a way of softening the mind, of releasing the bonds of conditioning that harness and bind us to familiar paths.'

Rudgwick was not completely sure he understood what the Manager had implied, so he smiled and changed the subject.

'Would you be so kind as to arrange a bouquet of flowers for each of the ladies in our party?'

'They are already in their rooms, sir. A welcome gift from the hotel. You will also find a bowl of exotic fruit and sweet water. I would avoid drinking from the taps, we are assured it has been tested but perhaps it might be wise for those of a delicate constitution and unused to its bitter taste to avoid it.

I sincerely hope you will enjoy your stay Mr Rudgwick.'

16. A SAVIOUR IN THE SLUMS.

Before they had set sail from England, the Viscount Chardwell, the Secretary of State, tried to forcibly appropriate as many medical supplies as possible for the hospital ships at anchor in the Thames still struggling to contain the final throes of the smallpox epidemic. But Jarret had told Chandler to lock them away.

And as soon as they had left the harbour, he ordered all clothes and overalls of the officers and crew to be boiled, and Chandler had kept an eagle eye out for any evidence of infection in the passengers.

He unlocked the medical cabinet hidden beneath the decking and carried them in an inconspicuous bag to his clinic.

The sight that greeted him made his heart sink and his anger rise. Queues of people, pregnant mothers, emaciated and disease ridden, skeletal men with infected limbs, stunned and traumatised, children and babies with swollen stomachs, listless and barely breathing without the strength to greet him as he made his way down the filthy back streets, damp and odorous with cracked pipes and discarded garbage, rats and detritus.

It was the silence that most alarmed him. Flesh and blood can scream, but when the spirit dies then so does hope, and there is no healing balm, no alchemy or magic that can ignite the soul.

In his youth, when he had trained in the hospitals in England, for those who hovered on the threshold of death there was an anger, a bitterness, a betrayal in their eyes. Almost an indignation.

But here, there was only resignation, defeat, an acceptance of their fate. A quiet submission. As if they had no right to life.

In the previous year when he had visited Bombay, the clinic had been invaded by journalists who descended like locusts seeking sensational stories during the epidemic.

Photographs and articles about the squalor, deprivation and lack of palliative care had made good copy around the world. But as soon as the print had run dry the world moved on. Callous in its disregard and finite in compassion.

One such article in an American newspaper he had kept and read often, to remind himself of the enormity of suffering and the ineluctable sweep of destiny.

It read:

"In the profound clamour of existence, there comes a time when one confronts the inevitability of resignation at death. Life, an intricate web of joy and sorrow, sometimes leaves souls defeated and weary.

When the burdens of existence become too heavy, and the relentless struggles of survival starve hope, individuals may find themselves standing at the precipice of surrender, gazing into the abyss of a seemingly helpless fate. Here is the terrifying story of a country sinking under the relentless and merciless waves of sorrow and discontent."

And another:

“The human experience is marked by resilience, an unyielding spirit that battles against the tides of adversity.

Yet, there are moments when weariness sets in, when the ceaseless demands of life chip away at the vigour within.

In these vulnerable instants, resignation may appear as a refuge, a perceived solace in the face of overwhelming challenges.

It's a contemplative surrender, an acknowledgment that the journey has become arduous, and the soul seeks respite from the relentless storms that batter its shores.”

Much was true. The resignation at death is not always a conscious decision. Rather, it can emerge as a gradual erosion of hope, a fading ember in the cold winds of despair. The human psyche, resilient as it may be, has its breaking point, where the weight of existence becomes unbearable. It's a surrender not necessarily to weakness but to the acknowledgment of one's limitations in the grand theatre of life.

Yet, Chandler believed that even in the solemnity of resignation, there exists a profound complexity, where the individual grapples with the paradox of surrendering to fate while yearning for liberation from the burdens that bind. It's a delicate dance between acceptance and resistance, a surrender that paradoxically embodies a silent rebellion against the harsh dictates of life.

Chandler walked along the quiet queue of helplessness. He had known abandonment. Poverty. He had experienced the profound and brutal human experience, the nature of suffering, the fragility of hope, and the enigma of mortality.

But he felt that even in the face of resignation, the human spirit, with its indomitable spark, continues to flicker in the vast expanse of eternity.

17. THAT EVENING.

The duchess was the first to arrive. The lounge was still, and only the sound of the ceiling fans broke the silence and filled the air with a welcome breeze.

Frau Köehler came down the stairs and walked over to sit by the duchess.

'Good evening, duchess. It seems we are the first.'

'I am always early, 'she said . 'Would you care for some tea?'

'Thank you.'

'It really is the finest I have tasted.'

They sat quietly, enjoying the salubrious surroundings, but a strange feeling of guilt seemed to pass between them, remembering the deprivation they had witnessed on the Dock at the harbour.

'I have been meaning to ask you about the conversation we were too tired to finish,' said the duchess. 'May I ask, did your past destructive relationship leave lasting scars? I hope not.'

'I was so very lonely,' she began.

'If any man showed even the slightest attention or affection, I would fall into his arms. It is so difficult to talk about,' said Frau Köehler. 'It makes me sound so immodest now, but in my wavering confidence I have always clung to a feeling that I had a value beyond my learning.

When you start a relationship. It's all about love is it not? Sharing support, encouragement, helping them to achieve their dreams, feeling you can make a difference to that person.

I was already bursting with talent, he told me, had had so many experiences, and achieved so much. What could he add?' he complained.

The only thing that was left was to diminish me. That would make a difference. Make him feel important, indispensable, make me dependant.

His very ordinariness, his so-called normality, was something he seemed proud of. Something to aspire to.

Slowly to seek his approval I stripped away any talents I had, to prove how much I loved the nothingness he was, until I was left an empty shell.'

She paused to take breath.

'We look for people who seem the same as us. But we change, do we not? We grow. It's inevitable. The balance changes. We need to find the courage to travel that uncertain path together, or alone. It is a very delicate tenuous chord that keeps people together and the human mind is so very fragile, so very, very fragile, full of anguish and desperation when it finally breaks.

But... no. It left no lasting scars...... I think.

With Frau Bergmeier's help I found a way forward. A way to heal.'

'For one so young,' said the duchess. 'You have suffered much my dear. We are told by those intrepid explorers of the human psyche that we are all self-reference beings.

We are always our first consideration. Perhaps to be otherwise demands a deeper understanding. A wisdom and understanding that transcends the confines of selfishness. It is a thorny path. But it is the beginning of a journey where we are trusted to hold the other person's dreams in our hands.

For some, their first instinct in the face of excellence is not to be inspired, but to feel insecure. Maybe that is why those with extraordinary talents seek out a solitary life so that they can speak their truth to the world, without encountering jealousy or envy and their attending negatives, as they weep and watch humanity brought to its knees by its own rapacious ego. Blind to how fractured the world has become. Oblivious that it is now an insatiable predator, at the mercy of its own appetite.'

Mr Rudgwick and Frau Bergmeier arrived and sat with them.

'Our apologies. We had talked for so long and had not noticed the time.'

They smiled at each other with an affection that was disarming, and Mr Rudgwick's face shone with a radiance they had not seen before.

~

A solitary figure appeared at the entrance. An old man, small and thin of stature, wearing a white sarong and a shawl draped across his head. He seemed to illuminate the room.

The kindness in his eyes put everyone at their ease.

'Forgive me. I am late,' he said.

'I am old, and time has little meaning for me now. I am Doctor Surinda.'

'May we offer you tea, Doctor Surinda?' asked the duchess.

'A glass of water. Thank you.'

They talked long into the evening and did not realise they had missed dinner, enraptured as they were by his extraordinary story.

'Perhaps you could first enlighten us how we appear to have all been brought together to meet you, as we have already become the dearest of friends,' said Frau Bergmeier, introducing herself.

'To begin with,' he said, 'I must regretfully inform you duchess, that the gentleman you so longed to meet, has already died. Our letters crossed on the ocean.'

'What unfortunate news! I am... quite devastated not to be able to meet such a remarkable man.'

'He was the kindest and most generous person I have ever met,' said Surinda. Turning to Rudgwick, he continued.

'And Mr Rudgwick, this is the same gentleman whose affairs you have come to conclude. He did not, as I originally thought, commit suicide... but was murdered.'

Rudgwick looked alarmed, his face turned pale and he was lost for words.

'And, Frau Bergmeier,' continued Surinda. 'I have here the deed to the mine which your grandfather leased to him, and which is now your sole property.'

Frau Köehler now realised why her dearest friend had chosen such a surprising destination.

'Forgive me, Frau Köehler. I believed I could conclude our business quickly and begin our adventure and I needed you with me.'

'Well, I never,' she said, and smiled.

As everyone was now aware of the reason for each other's visit, Rudgwick Informed them of the Colonel's unfortunate life, and the arrangements his firm was requested to organise in passing on the proceeds of the mine to his family, and his wish to remain anonymous.

'Perhaps,' said Frau Bergmeier, 'you could tell us how this gentleman's extraordinary journey began, Doctor Surinda?'

Doctor Surinda collected his thoughts like one assembling a collection of painful memories.

'The owner of the mine, your grandfather, had sent instructions from Cape Town that I should meet the Colonel's ship and afford him every assistance. I had been recommended by a Doctor I knew who was working in the military hospital in Africa where the Colonel was recovering. He warned me that he had been badly disfigured and to keep him away from prying eyes as much as was possible.'

'Tea?' suggested the duchess, with the confidence that it was the answer to every Englishman's problem.

'Thank you,' said Surinda. 'After he arrived, I assembled a small work force, sufficient provisions and with several mules we made our way up the mountain.

They worked for many months in scorching temperatures.

When the monsoon arrived, the mine would flood, and the work was slow. After a while it became evident to him that not much profit was to be made with such a meagre team. One by one they began to leave, complaining that the work was hard and repulsed by this grotesque but gentle master.

He fell into a deep fever which raged for many weeks, and we feared he would not survive. I offered to bring more qualified doctors to him, but he refused, saying, "It makes no matter."

He had sweet water and provisions and eventually seemed to recover.

Children would play in the mountains and see this strange white creature who lived in the cave. But when they returned at night to taunt and throw stones at him, they found him turned to black, and they fled in terror, not knowing, because they were children, it was the coal dust from the mine.

The moonlight can play strange tricks with your eyes in the Maharashtra.

Soon the legend spread of the terrifying Black and White God who lived in the cave, and all were fearful to go into the mountains.

"Let them fear me," he would say. "Then they will leave me in peace."

As is often the way amongst innocent people, the rumours spread and many began to believe that the cave was the home of some unknown monster who wished to harm Kali, a much misunderstood and maligned Goddess, and who they mistakenly believed reigned over the sexual licentiousness and bacchanalian erotic orgies that were practised by the prostitutes in the village, who had sought refuge in the cave from their cruel handlers.

Please forgive my frankness ladies.

They would merely visit the cave and bring food to the man who had comforted and protected them.

But some will always want to think the worst of people and project their own suppressed desires onto others, to assuage their guilt and pretences of virtue.

Then... the gold was discovered.'

'The gold? ' said Frau Bergmeier.

'Yes,' said Surinda.

He continued his story and told them that he would journey to the mine every month and secretly bring the gold to Bombay where it would be weighed and valued.

He would deposit it at the bank and send half to England, through the practice of Mr Rudgwick, which was to be given to his family on the understanding that they never try to discover their anonymous benefactor.

'The other half I was to distribute, at his request, to the local village for the elders to build schools and a hospital for the children, making me promise I would never tell them where it came from.

The village thrived, but over the years the elders became arrogant and proud and resented that they were not able to go into the mountains.

One night they gathered with torches and spears and swarmed into the mountains at moonrise, driving him into

the cave, mutilating him and leaving him a charred and burning inferno.
Horrifying! Terrifying,' said Surinda, wiping his brow.

'Forgive me for asking Doctor, but this will be important to my family. How did he discover the vein of gold?' asked Frau Bergmeier.

'That is a story...... difficult to tell. I have never revealed it. Not to a single soul.'

His hands were shaking, trembling, as he drank a tumbler of water.

'I'm sorry,' he swallowed. 'I have a dry mouth.'

He looked at them all.

'Mysterious things can happen in the mountains, but all of this is true. All of it.' He took another gulp of water. And then related to them the fearful events of that night.

'One evening', he told them; 'Faulkner had appeared. He was standing in the doorway while a storm raged, lightning struck the trees and the sky seemed to bleed.

Was he Man or Beast?'

"All is well," he said.

'But his voice was deep within his throat and rattling in his mouth. Like the lost language of Trimurti.

His face was painted blue and yellow and goat horns cradled his head. Wreaths of vines hung from his shoulders and white feathers cascaded from his waist.

"Come in a week," he said, "there will be gold."

“Are you well?” I asked, but he seemed distracted, distant. As if... floating in the air. Yes... floating.

Then his eyes, iridescent, deep as purple... washed over me...through me... and the words seemed to pour from his mouth like liquid sound.

"The goats," he whispered, in a tongue I did not recognize but strangely understood.

"The goats of the cave, translucent, blue and green, led me in a bright darkness to the veins of gold. Their song was beautiful, and they sang of wonders waiting beyond the vein. Emeralds, rubies and sapphires, whispering in the rocks, calling my name. They placed horns upon my head and coloured me yellow, blue and red, and led me through the twelve walls of rock, which fell away like tumours from the earth to pools of dancing diamonds. And my laughter filled the cave and echoed down the mountains, making children, beast and fowl flee in terror.”

Tears ran down his cheeks and streams of colour dripped onto his chest.

"The old goat’s song echoed around the cave and led me to a deeper darkness," he said. "As they walked, they sang."

"Do not ask us to tell you of life. Each painful day bleeds onto the next recreating the festering wound called wisdom, from which you never recover. From which you quake in awe at its enormity and end your days as perplexed as children, damaged, broken, submissive.”

"The goats turned, and gazing at the ground, they continued."

"What do you want of us? You think because we are old, we have answers for your journey? That we know where the abyss is into which you might fall on the road you travel?

The sun rises and the sun sets. And we do not know if it will rise again or where it goes, and what is the purpose of darkness?

One thing is certain, without it, you cannot see the stars."

The song carried gently on the air. Intoxicating colours of sound. The goats stumbled and stopped and held him in their gaze.

"Why does the ocean hold so many tears? Are they the tears of the abandoned? The dispossessed? Denied, because they wanted something? To be Gods? What must we do to earn our place in Paradise? To be the angels of the sun. The wings of the Moon. The unbeings without breath. They know what awaits us.
Rest. Rest," they sang. "There is only the alchemy of chemicals. The mystery of form. An eternity of atoms.

The goats walked on, and I followed, deeper into the depths of the cave, as if in ecstasy, descending to a womb of ice, and ascending through the softest silk into the clouds.

Come tomorrow. All will be well," he said.

And as he turned away, he disappeared into the raging storm. That was the last I saw of him.

Until I found him in the cave.'

Surinda stared into the distance.

'Deranged? Possessed? Honestly? He seemed.... transmuted.

Perhaps the most astounding revelation,' said Surinda, 'was that when I looked up, having turned my face away in fear, his wounds.... had healed. His face... once deformed almost beyond recognition was... restored, and now, was radiant, and when his eyes fell upon you it was as if some warm summer breeze had soothed you completely, renewed and reinvigorated you. As if, by some miracle, his goodness... had healed him from the inside.'

He sat for a while in silence.

'The gold flowed for many years. He would leave it at the entrance of the cave, and I would leave provisions. If he had no food, he would eat plants and herbs, and drink sweet water from the mountain streams. I would often hear singing coming from the cave and all seemed good and well... until that fateful night.

The villagers in their naivety had not seen what lay before their eyes. Consumed as they were with fear and earthly blindness, they had slaughtered the eternal, primal and immortal gift they had been offered.

As the village deteriorated, they were filled with remorse and regret, and felt they had offended the God in the cave, so they built a statue to him in the centre of the village.'

'Is the statue still standing?' asked Rudgwick.

'Oh yes, sir. After he had been slaughtered, we waited several days for the frenzy to subside and went to retrieve the body and take him by cart to the water's edge and burn him on a funeral pyre. The night was clear and the waters calm. The flames burned bright on the sand and wood was plentiful. Many came with torches and stayed until dawn to watch the shedding.

And once the skull had exploded from the heat and his soul was released... all was scattered on the wind.

Some weeks later I returned to the cave and searched for the gold and glistening rocks to continue his legacy, but...none were found. Only silence and darkness. And the goats who watched from the mountain.

Months later, when the village had fallen into ruin, the children, now playing at the feet of the statue they had built to honour him, ran screaming to the elders to come and see! The statue... had turned to gold and the entire village stood in wonder and worshipped at his feet.

Soon the legend spread and thousands from all around would come to see the miracle. And the village prospered once again.

And many said at night when the wind blew through the mountains, the statue would sing. A soft celestial song that made all that heard it weep and laugh. And the strange goat creatures would gather on the mountain top.

Dare I ask?' said Surinda, almost to himself, ' Were they.... his progeny? Or just another mystery of The Maharashtra?

In the moonlight the statue was white, then black, and at sunrise, turned again to gold.'

They sat in silence, watching Surinda, who stared at the floor. His lips were pale and his eyes red. He was frail and weak. Exhausted.

Frau Bergmeier rose and sat next to him.

'Doctor. I feel I must see the cave with my own eyes. And then we can seal it and leave it in peace.'

Doctor Surinda nodded, and she placed a hand gently on his arm.

He smiled.

'I will make arrangements.'

~

Before they retired and Doctor Surinda had left, Rudgwick asked if the villagers who had murdered the Colonel had been arrested.

As he helped him into his cart, Surinda explained that the elders responsible for his death gave themselves up to the authorities.

Rudgwick found this unusual, but when it was explained that here they feared retribution, not from the State, but from an omnipotent deity. If they did not pay the price in this life, they would pay for it in their next incarnation.

The judgement was complicated because the Colonel had written a letter before his death saying that if he came to harm from another's hand they should not be punished, because they would be doing him a service.

As noble as it was, it made little difference to the sentence. They received life in prison rather than death.

When the elders learned that they had killed the person who had been so generous to their village, they were filled with remorse and were inconsolable. They refused food, and after many months of suffering, they died of starvation.

The next few days were difficult for the group. They didn't venture out but stayed within the hotel, as the memories of everything they had learned troubled them all deeply.

18. LONDON ST JAMES.

In the dimly lit rooms of Sir Ranulph's club, a heavy pallor of consternation hung in the air. The flickering candlelight cast elongated shadows on the oak-panelled walls, mirroring the sombre disquiet etched across Malbraid's face. His stoic demeanour, a bastion of legal rectitude, betrayed a disquietude stirred by the unfolding tumult of the Boer War displayed in the capital's newspapers.

The Times and the London Gazette lay scattered across his mahogany desk, each headline a lamentation that resonated with the echoes of bereaved parents. This distant conflict on foreign soil hung heavily over the hallowed halls of British homes. Sir Ranulph, a man accustomed to the measured tones of courtroom oratory, found himself grappling with the grief that reverberated from the ink-blackened columns of the papers.

His club, a sanctuary for his advancing years, was thick with the scent of aged leather-bound volumes, yet, on this eve, the comforting scent seemed tainted by the acrid ink of war correspondents, chronicling the harrowing tales of lost sons and broken families. The sanctity of familial bonds, once sacrosanct now lay fractured on the battlefield; their echoes reaching even the confines of his oasis of calm.

In another column he perused the damning accusations of yet another attempted assassination on the sovereign herself at Windsor. A frown etched deeper lines upon his face. The spectre of regicide and sinister treason cast a shadow upon the very foundations of the British Empire.

In the dim glow of the candlelight, Sir Ranulph wrote into the early hours of a wretched morning, drafting missives and petitions that sought justice for the fallen and redress for the aggrieved. His legal acumen, a beacon of hope in these turbulent times, stood resolute along side the tempest of public affront. The ink-stained pages bore witness to his fervent efforts to navigate the corridors of justice, seeking solace for those who had sacrificed their kin in the crucible of war.

Being well past the age when youthful vigour leant his arguments the gift of persuasion, enjoying the fruits of a rapier-like intellect, he nonetheless endeavoured, in the absence of Rudgwick, whose presence he sorely missed, to deal with the urgent matters at hand with as much clarity as he could muster.

He found himself ensnared in a tapestry of war, grief, and the spectre of regicidal intrigue, and the burden lay heavy on him. The ink on his legal documents mirrored the indelible stain that the War had left upon the collective conscience of a nation that promised to echo through the annals of history with the weight of a thousand lost sons and the unsettling murmurings of rebellion.

One such missive he was reluctant to write was to Lady Faulkner. Until he was informed in full of the entire misfortune that had befallen the Colonel he would refrain from communication with the gracious Lady.

Although no doubt the military would have notified her of his unfortunate and possibly untimely death, his heart sank at the grief that she and her dear family must inevitably endure.

19. THE JOURNEY TO THE MOUNTAINS.

After a few days Surinda returned to take Rudgwick, Frau Bergmeier, and Frau Köehler, who had both agreed to accompany her to his practice outside his village, and then take mules up the mountain to the cave.

The duchess had left the day earlier travelling by train to Delhi for her meeting with the Viceroy. It would be at least a month before she returned by ship to England and they all hoped that they would meet again, had promised to stay in communication, and were all sad to see her leave.

It was a slow journey for the group. Surinda's friend, Rajah, had offered to drive the other cart to help but refused to journey further into the mountains.

At midday they pulled the carts into a shady grove and unpacked the food Surinda had brought.

The bird song was deafening as Frau Bergmeier looked up at the sun shining through the leaves of tall trees surrounding the glade.

'That is a sacred Banyan tree, 'said Surinda. 'Three hundred years old. It has been here during many occupations and no doubt has many stories.'

'And that one?' asked Frau Köehler.

'That is an old Peepal tree. Some other trees are more than three thousand years old. By lighting a diya under it and offering water to the plant we can rid ourselves of all

Doshas.The long strings that hang from it are hung there by wives praying their husbands will have a long life.'

'That string is quite short,' said Rudgwick.

'Then perhaps it needs no explanation,' chuckled Surinda. 'They are all mystical and all worshipped.'

Rudgwick suddenly went very pale.

'What is it Mr Rudgwick?' asked Surinda.

'It's strange,' he said. 'Very strange.'

He sat down and looked at the ground feeling perplexed.

'When I was a child, I had a recurring dream. I was a very large Salamander - well fed and healthy. I was climbing out of a large indoor swimming pool and scuttled into the shadows. The pool was opulent, of green dappled marble, as were the huge green marble columns which surround it. I felt I belonged there. There was no fear.

The sun shone through a far-off door, fierce and relentless, but in the water, it was cool and pleasant.'

'We have had many incarnations to bring us to this life,' said Rajah, lisping through the cracked teeth he had left and smiling broadly. 'A human birth is very rare. You would have earned it with merit.'

Frau Bergmeier walked over to Rudgwick and sat beside him.

'Perhaps you were a favoured pet, Mr Rudgwick, in the palace of a King,' Frau Köehler touched his shoulder gently and smiled.

'Or an ancient God,' she added.

'Much loved,' Frau Bergmeier said. 'I shall now always call you, my little Salamander.'

Rudgwick smiled. 'In which case I feel compelled to call you, Frau Fiddle.'

She laughed.

'But what shall I be called?' said Frau Köehler. An old insecurity surfacing and feeling rather excluded.

They both said they must give that some thought because it was important, but assured her it would be affectionate.

Surinda began to tidy away the picnic and Rajah placed the blankets in the back of his cart, helping Frau Bergmeier up onto her seat.

'There are many mysteries in the human psyche, Mr Rudgwick, we dismiss with alacrity. Many voices speak to us of times long past that make us what we are and speak of what we must learn. Here, in Asia, it is called "Karma".'

'It is an amazing country. And their devotion is unique,' said Rudgwick.

'Well, India has somehow imprinted on the mind of the world a monopoly on enlightenment. That only here can one transcend this earthly prison. It is not so.

One only needs to walk through our golden temples, behemoths of opulence, and spend a while in the slums of Dharavi to see that we have the same unjust imbalances as many other nations.'

They continued their journey, enjoying the sights and smells of an unfamiliar land.

20. DELHI.

Despite the difference in titles, the duchess should nonetheless have been afforded a better degree of respect, but the Viceroy was a patronising, smug little man, and no doubt on the Indian subcontinent would have been considered tall, but towering over him with her immense stature she was an intimidating presence. So, it did not surprise her that, in order to retain some semblance of masculine authority, he resorted to the underhand tactics that some men do when threatened by a superior feminine intellect -he ignored her, and kept her waiting for nearly two hours.

In the stifling heat of Delhi, the duchess found herself ensconced in the waiting room of the Viceroy's residence, a locale far removed from the genteel ambiance of Bombay she had reluctantly bid adieu.

Her frustration, palpable like the oppressive warmth that enveloped her, simmered beneath the veneer of aristocratic composure.

As she languished amidst the uncomfortable wooden furniture, the duchess pondered the delicate equilibrium of authority.

Men of supposed eminence, the Viceroys and their ilk, were but fragile souls, their confidence dangling precariously, susceptible to the whims of politics and power plays. She observed, with an astute eye honed by social intricacies, the subtleties of influence and insecurity that characterised the chambers of authority she had also witnessed in the halls of Parliament which seemed a world away.

While the Viceroy attended to matters of imperial import, the duchess found herself yearning for the camaraderie of her Bombay acquaintances. The vibrant conversations and cultural soirees aboard the ship seemed like distant echoes in the cavernous halls of Delhi's bureaucratic machinery.

But the business at hand demanded her presence in this alien environment, for a time severing the threads of connection she had meticulously woven and cherished on the long voyage from England and in her short stay in Bombay, the Empire's second city.

Draped in unsuitable layers of clothing, she battled not only the sweltering Delhi heat, but also the relentless assault of persistent flies, which were most irritating. The ornate ceiling fans whirred above, their rhythmic hum blending with the ambient sounds of an administrative beehive.

Each passing moment heightened her awareness of the stark contrast between the refined elegance of Bombay and the bureaucratic rigmarole of the capital.

Amidst the discomfort, the duchess grappled with a subtle realization - her own resilience mirrored the fortitude of the men in positions of authority. They too, like her, navigated through the complexities of circumstance, their confidence a delicate façade concealing the intricate dance of political machinations.

And so, in that waiting room, under the weight of unsuitable attire and the relentless drone of bureaucracy, the duchess reflected on the fragility that bound them all, like players in an elaborate performance where the script was ever-changing, and the stakes remained high.

As the hours slipped by, the duchess found herself enveloped in a contemplative solitude that peeled away the layers of aristocratic stoicism. Her own vulnerabilities, usually shrouded by the opulence of societal privilege, surfaced in the starkness of that bureaucratic chamber. The weight of societal expectations, like an intricate corset, constricted her freedom, making her acutely aware of the subtle battles she waged daily.

The echoes of discontent resonated not only within the chambers of her own heart but also in the collective sighs of women across the strata of society. She couldn't dismiss the persistent murmurings of change that reverberated beyond the confines of the waiting room. Women, weary of silent subjugation, yearned to assert themselves in ways that transcended the constraints of subtlety.

The duchess, an unwitting observer of these societal undercurrents, recognized the silent rebellion that simmered beneath the veils and crinolines. In the gestures and glances she discerned the quiet defiance of those who dared to challenge the established norms.

As she grappled with her own vulnerabilities, she pondered the intricate balance between tradition and progress. The desire for change, palpable and potent. The discontent of women, stifled by convention, sought avenues of expression beyond the ornate walls that confined them.

In the quiet moments of reflection, amidst the heat, the irritating flies and the ceaseless whir of ceiling fans, the

duchess found herself sympathising with the yearning for autonomy that transcended her own station.

As she awaited the Viceroy's audience, the duchess couldn't help but feel a subtle kinship with the unsung heroines who, in their own ways, sought to rewrite the script of their lives.

'You've caught me at an inconvenient time, Duchess Beaufort,' said the Viceroy gruffly, opening his door as two subordinates scuttled away down the long corridor juggling missives and scrolls like performers in a circus.

'I'm having to deal with these wretched riots in Madras, so I'll have to keep our meeting brief. I now have the correspondence from Parliament and the letter you sent me from Bombay.'

'Are you in a position to help these unfortunate women?' said the duchess.

'Probably, but please bear in mind that things are splitting at the seams here. Sometimes making love is the only blasted comfort a man can get in this infernal climate.'

'Somehow, Viceroy, I don't think love comes into the equation.'

'Oh, come now, you are a woman of the world and know the pressure everyone is under.'

'You will have no argument from me about anything consensual Viceroy, but state sponsored prostitution is morally repugnant. If these unfortunate women contract a disease from our soldiers they are thrown into prison until they are cured. This does not however seem to apply to the male population who are free to reinfect any future, compelled, and unfortunate women working in the chaklas.'

'They accept the money do they not?'

'What little is given to them,' scoffed the duchess. 'The inequalities are enforced by the Empire. Perhaps it is not wise to add to the atrocities we have already committed in the name of unity?'

He looked up with indignation.

'Do you honestly believe madam that the majority of Indians would have been treated better by the princes than by the British?'

'Maybe not. We'll never know. Perhaps when they do have unity we'll discover. I wonder what will happen then?'

'A blood bath.'

The discussion was becoming heated, and the duchess thought it best to return to the reason for her visit.

'I'm sure if we leave affairs of India in your capable hands any problems will be overcome with the efficiency we would expect from such a notable official.'

The Viceroy was not sure if he had detected a slight undertone of sarcasm.

'Quite.'

'The European women, as I was about to say, are brought here under false pretences with the offer of a better life. And that should be considered criminal.'

He sighed.

‘Indeed. I will look into it.’

‘Thank you. I shall report to Mr Madge in Parliament that you have graciously offered your help.’

He smiled embarrassingly and lit a cigar.

’Do you mind?’

‘Not at all.’

He continued.

‘With regard to the other matter, I'm afraid you must contact the local authorities in Bombay if you want more funding for Mr Chandler. Everything I spend here must be accounted for.

One must be ruthless when governing our Colonies.'

‘I think when most of the military and local population are wiped out with cholera, syphilis and gonorrhoea, there may be little population left to govern.’

He was becoming exasperated.

‘I believe,’ she continued, 'Mr Chandler brings these medical supplies at his own expense, which I'm sure you'll agree is outrageous.’

‘We are at the mercy of government! When new laws are passed, we shall enact them. And now... I really must get on. Forgive me.’

‘Thank you for your time, viceroy. I am delighted that our Colony is being cared for by someone with such compassion, and who is a shining light of Christian values to our protestant missionaries’.

He made no answer.

She left the room and descended the stairs like a Galleon in full sail. He slammed the door.

'Bloody women!'

The duchess climbed into her waiting carriage muttering to herself that despite her best intentions she was unable to resist veiled sarcasm when confronted with pomposity and arrogance, and pondered why, when bastions of authority confront themselves, it has all the subtlety of two battleships ramming upon the high seas.

The smell of his cigar still lingered on her clothes and reminded her of after dinner gatherings in her youth, when her father would stand with an oversized cigar in his mouth, like an infant's pacifier, or a mini-obelisk.

On her long and arduous journey back to Bombay she had ample time to reflect on the lessons that life had taught her.

As she had grown older, she found the thing she valued most in life was character. She had known exalted pillars of the establishment, in the government, the clergy and in the judiciary who possessed levels of pomposity, and corruption which was breathtaking in its immorality. And in contrast, often amongst the unfortunate, the downtrodden and destitute, or even the criminals of the underworld, she had found a level of honour and moral rectitude that would have put the Pope to shame.

Inequity, she thought, is more readily obvious to the trained eye, whilst humility often lies beneath layer upon layer of self-effacing modesty. And, as one that always questioned her behaviour and attitudes, she considered whether she might have misjudged Mr Chandler.

Despite his arrogance and haughty demeanour, the viceroy was not unaware of the difficulties under British rule and had witnessed the complexities of both economic growth and social injustice. He was cognisant of the fact that the British Raj, while contributing to the economic development of the region, inflicted a considerable degree of cruelty on the local population. The oppressive policies and exploitative practices implemented by the colonial administration had left a lasting impact on the lives of the people.

He walked out onto his balcony and sat watching the gardeners tend to the debris caused by the recent monsoon.

Uprooted trees and crumbling walls, flooded walkways, and snakes and land monitors washed down from the mountains. The sweet smell of rotting fruit and the dampness in his shirt made him change frequently, as a relentless humidity permeated the rooms, and the ceiling fans made him shiver.

He watched the young boys childishly playing with fallen leaves and broken bracken, sweeping the petals of flowers away from the paths and into the gutters.

One of the stark manifestations of cruelty was the economic exploitation imposed on the indigenous population. The introduction of cash-crop cultivation and the emphasis on export-oriented industries led to the displacement of traditional agrarian practices. The local farmers, who had sustained themselves for generations, found themselves subjugated to the demands of an imperialistic economic system, causing widespread poverty and destitution.

The viceroy walked to his desk and sorted through some of the documents that needed his attention.

The social fabric of Bombay, as the duchess would no doubt discover, also bore the scars of British cruelty. Discriminatory policies and racial hierarchies had created a divided society.

The elites enjoyed privileges and preferential treatment, enforced with breathtaking arrogance, while the local populace faced systemic discrimination fuelling resentment and laying the foundation for social unrest.

Moreover, the Empire displayed a callous disregard for the cultural sensitivities and traditions of the indigenous people. The imposition of western norms and values undermined local customs, eroding the richness of India's cultural heritage. This cultural insensitivity further widened the gap between the rulers and the ruled, fostering an environment of discontent and resistance.

The legal and political system also reflected the cruelty of British rule. Unjust laws, biased judiciary, and lack of political representation marginalised the voices of the local population. The absence of a fair and inclusive governance structure allowed the British authorities to wield unchecked power, leading to widespread human rights abuses and denial of basic freedoms.

The viceroy watched as the duchess's carriage trundled lazily through the open gates of the residence.

He also knew that the scars left by colonial rule would echo through the coming decades, shaping the trajectory of India's history and would no doubt contribute to the larger narrative of India's future struggles.
But for the moment he kept his concerns to himself. He was answerable to a greater power.

21. THE CAVE.

The journey up the mountain path had taken longer than anticipated. The light was fading and they were anxious that they may have to spend the night in the cave.

'I have brought sufficient provisions and blankets. It is peaceful in the mountains now,' Surinda reassured them. They dismounted and he lit tapers for them all.

'The cave is not very deep. I will lay out some food and prepare a fire for when you return.'

'You will not accompany us?' said Frau Köehler with alarm.

'I have seen it. It is only small.'

The three walked into the cave.

What was left of the light had now faded and the tapers cast shadows on the walls. A sweet smell of flowers was carried on the breeze and the air was cold, at first a welcome change from the scorching sun, but they now began to shiver.

In the darkness they could not see the end of the cave and seemed to walk for a long time. Frau Bergmeier held her taper to the wall to see if she could detect anything other than coal or rock.

'There is nothing here,' she said. 'No vein of gold, alas.'

Their breathing became laboured.

Within the confines of the cave and the incessant and oppressive heat they were becoming light-headed.

The shortness of air made the tapers flicker and Rudgwick had to prevent Frau Köehler from stumbling in the fading light.

A sudden rock fall from the depths of the cave made them turn with fear.

Slowly from the shadows the glistening shapes of horns appeared and moved towards them. They edged back, stumbling, but their legs had turned to stone, as the herd's breath echoed around the cave. Their eyes fixed upon them. Merciless. Lascivious. Their mouths salivating and drooling foam.

As they reared up on hind legs, their immense and weeping manhood struck terror in their hearts as the herd fell upon them tearing their clothes to shreds, and screaming in rage and ecstasy, deafening their ears as the vicious carnal attack continued through the long night, until the dawn, when his progeny turned and slowly, spent and blood-stained, limped back into the depths of the cave as their howls were carried on the mountain wind.

~

Left writhing on the cave floor, in agony, they reached out in quiet desperation as their bruised bodies intertwined. They released a passion so intense it was difficult to know where one started and the other ended; satisfying each other in ways that words fail.

Lips drank lips and chartered well the surface of their skin. Innocence was lost in a sacred dance, and burning arrows flew between their pierced and purple wounds, submitting, as they bled in sacrifice as flesh was torn in pain and pleasure, willingly condemned to feast on dripping blood and open mouths where each would enter with violent desire.

Silence fell.

As the tapers burned out and the first rays of dawn bled into the cave, in agony, they staggered to their feet and tried to wrap what clothes they could find to cover their nakedness. They helped each other from the cave and stumbling over broken horns, blood, and matted hair, they crawled out into the morning light.

They saw that Doctor Surinda had fallen asleep and mountain goats were eating the food he had laid out.

After throwing stones at them they wrapped blankets around themselves, huddled together for warmth, and fell into a deep sleep.

~

They slept all the rest of the day and through the next night. Still exhausted, they stirred at dawn.

Doctor Surinda was tending the mules.

'I tried to wake you, but somehow you were deeply unconscious, delirious, and I thought it better that I let you rest. I mixed a healing drink from the herbs of the mountain and gently dripped it into your mouths and slowly you became calm, but still you slept.'

They looked at each other with a mixture of relief and shame. They were hot and sweating profusely and they eased the blankets a little. They looked down at their clothes. And far from being ripped to pieces, they were untouched. Unblemished. Unchanged.

In disbelief, none dared mention what they believed had happened. Quietly they walked about lost in wonder.

'The winds are strong in the mountains and carry spores from many plants and herbs which still remain a mystery,' said Surinda.

'If you have seen all you need, we should return. The path downhill will make for an easier journey.'

Rugwick helped Frau Bergmeier and Frau Köehler into the saddle, and mounting his mule, followed Doctor Surinda down the mountain side.

Glancing back, they saw the morning sun, now fully risen, cast rays of burning light into the mouth of the cave, and flocks of goats, now watching from the mountain, held them in their gaze.

22. WELLINGBOROUGH. ENGLAND.

Faulkner Manor.

In the dimly lit drawing room of their ancestral estate, Lady Faulkner sat holding a chilling missive that had arrived bearing news of her husband and his unfortunate fate on the treacherous Zulu battlefields of Isandlwana.

The flickering candlelight cast shadows on her face as she read the solemn words, each line a tolling bell of despair.

Her hands trembled.

Cradling the parchment like a fragile artefact of sorrow she walked to the window.

Gazing out at the grounds of their estate which now seemed empty and as hollow as her heart, the weight of widowhood draped over her shoulders as she grappled with the impending darkness that loomed over her family.

Yet, the stoicism of a woman moulded by the empire enveloped her, and she hid her profound grief beneath a veneer of quiet strength.

For the sake of her two sons, heirs to a legacy forged in imperial sacrifice, Lady Faulkner donned the mask of composure. Her eyes, pools of unshed tears, betrayed the depth of her devastation, but in the hallowed halls of the estate, she bore her burden in the stillness of her grieving heart. The echoes of distant battle cries seemed to resonate within her, as she knew she must shield her sons from the harsh reality that had befallen their family.

From her earliest childhood Lady Faulkner had learned the ways of womanhood. The unacceptable face of emotions. The silent suffrage. The cold indifference to the capricious whims of life.

But she also knew the quiet places in her heart, where the banished dreams of youth recoiled from the stern features of a mother made of stone; the matriarchs of moral rectitude, the pillars of defiance and self-abnegation that supported the might of the British Empire.

Her dear friend, Millicent Fawcet, had been a rock of support both before and after her marriage. Fawcet was a strong, ambitious woman and highly intelligent. She often expressed her disapproval of the militant attitudes towards equality developing amongst certain groups of women, and feared that the cause would be lost if they alienated parliament. She was convinced a more subtle and perhaps more cunning approach would yield better results.

In the quiet of the evening, they would often discuss the benefits that society could gain if they were afforded the freedoms they craved.

As it happened, Miss Fawcett was due to visit that evening and Lady Faulkner was glad to have someone with whom she shared a common bond, to be able to unburden her deepest feelings of sorrow and apprehension.

Emotional repression had profound effects on women's mental and physical well-being. Standards of propriety, modesty, and decorum suppressed any outward displays of emotion.

Denied the freedom to openly express their feelings, women often grappled with internalised turmoil, leading to heightened stress and anxiety.

The stifling of genuine emotions contributed to a sense of isolation and internal conflict, as women struggled to reconcile society's expectations with their authentic selves and became a conduit for unexpressed feelings.

Headaches, fatigue, and other stress-related ailments became commonplace and ridiculed, serving as tangible manifestations of the emotional burdens women carried.

Marriage in particular bore the brunt, as women found themselves unable to communicate openly with their husbands. This lack of emotional intimacy contributed to a society that valued appearances over genuine emotional needs.

Lady Eleanora Faulkner had been a good wife, a silent partner in an arranged future. Without complaint she had been crafted to fit the role demanded of her.

She loved her husband deeply; but as a stranger, content with the implied affection of his hand upon her shoulder, and a contented sigh as he left her bed.

The literature of the time poignantly depicted female characters that grappled with the consequences of stifled emotions.

Literary works served as a mirror reflecting the demands of appearances over genuine feelings. The toll they took on women's well-being and their mental health stifled any individual growth. For women were expected to embody the virtues of purity, submissiveness, and selflessness. Pushing them into the shadows of their own landscape and seriously affecting their own mental stability.

The paintings hanging on the walls of Millicent Fawcet's friends by tortured female artists struggling with the tourniquets of life were a strange combination of light and dark. Of shadows, revealing secret intent. An expression of hubris. The aesthetics of conquest and domination. The unexplored world of sexual depravity, reckless and violent, given licence to express the forbidden, the repressed, the subdued.

The loss of control at the mercy of the gothic intellectual and the bestial monster salivating at the mouth of lust, at the threshold of debauchery.

These paintings were controversial and rejected with disgust in an age still struggling with the meaning of freedom and liberation. Lady Faulkner found them disturbing and unsettling.

"Dreams and aspirations are a luxury few can afford, my dear Eleanora," Millicent had said. while walking arm in arm together through the crowded streets of London.

"The indulgence of contemplating the meaning of existence is left to the artist, the beggar, or the idle aristocracy. The rest of us are shackled to a daily grind of service and duty."

The governments bleed what they can from their people, and the church sedates them with fairytales. We place our trust in a higher authority we cannot see and an institution that is self-serving. Like a dragon that eats its own tail, it consumes itself, leaving us destitute and desolate, inwardly and outwardly, barren and disillusioned, begging for crumbs from the tables of the mighty, the rich, and the powerful, who are always terrified that the public will one day realise that they are the resource that nurtures their nest.

But how pathetic are our protestations. How weak we think we are.

What a mess we have made of life. How pompous and arrogant have we become in our long littleness.

And when the entire edifice comes crashing down, as it has in the past and will again, we rebuild it in the same way, with the same tools, and worship at the feet of this insanity, with its robes of glory and uniforms of homogeneity. Feeding our desperate need to belong. To have purpose. To find meaning."

Supported by the tenacious and daring nature of Miss Fawcet, her warmth and affection, it was a certainty that Lady Faulkner would face the coming darkness with fortitude and a resolute stoicism, forged on the anvil of empire.

23. RETURN TO BOMBAY.

Surinda could sense, as they journeyed back to Bombay, a disquiet and unease in his companions. A darkness and fear had descended which troubled them. To ease the silence, he sang gently to himself.

'Is your practice busy Doctor Surinda?' asked Rudgwick, but he continued to stare blankly at the road ahead as if searching for answers.

'Oh yes, sir. Very busy. I was given many opportunities when I was younger. I was fortunate, due to the blessed Sir Robert Grant, to study medicine at the new Grant Medical College.'

He affectionately produced a fading sepia photograph from his pocket and showed it to him.

'I also studied ayurvedic medicine which was becoming less popular because of the pressure from the Empire.

And of course, the temptations as a young man to study western medicine and earn 30 rupees a month was exciting, but it was a credit to the British that they also recognized we possessed in India local genius. Ayurvedic medicine has existed for many, many years.

The world is beautiful, Mr Rudgwick. It is a magic shadow show in a box, whose candle is the sun.'

He chuckled.

They rode on in silence and the landscape changed from rocks and hills to endless pastures, green and vibrant.

'There is so much beauty here,' said Rudgwick. 'The fields are as deep and green as an emerald sea.

We are told by our poets that England is an emerald isle, and maybe once it was, but it often seems as if it is covered in a mysterious melancholy mist. I was born into a land of steam and grime, choking in the smoke of dark machines where sometimes the putrid smog of London would hug the buildings like a suffocating cloak, like a gracious lady slowly fading into a darker age.'

'It is a feast for the eyes, yes, but often, Mr Rudgwick, such effulgent, lush and verdant pastures are a sign of over-fertilising. Beautiful, but hazardous to the soil and wildlife.'

Surinda gently urged the oxen on. They had become slow and closed their eyes as the heat of the day beat relentlessly in waves upon their backs.

'And what of the Colonel, did he visit often?'

'Not so often, but when he did, I would give him chai. Ashwagandha chai. It is almost six thousand years old, used as an Ayuvedic Rasayana. Of course, he did not know this, but...it was a kind deceit. It kept him calm and has many, many good properties. You see, he had a distrust of all medicine. Even though it saved his life in Africa it left him brutally deformed and in constant pain, so he didn't wish to be treated. In my village many allow you to treat them so long as you promise not to make them well. Never to cure them.

You see, their illness is their identity, and they are reluctant to give it up; but it was not so with him. He just refused treatment.

"Let things come to a natural end," he would say.

If food was late, he would eat grasses and herbs and drink sweet water from the streams. I couldn't tell what effect they had on him but there are many potent plants and shrubs in the mountains collected since the time of the ancients and even now by unregistered practitioners, and the waters of the mountain streams have an unusual effect on some people.'

Rudgwick didn't answer but gazed out at the sea of green.

'You seem troubled, Mr Rudgwick?'

'I am slowly beginning to understand how mysterious India is. It has a way of making you disbelieve your senses.'

'Our senses are not always a reliable indicator and do not always serve us well. Our perceptions are limited if we only believe what we can see and hear, taste or touch. Sometimes in our lives, portals open which beckon to a different realm. It is as if we have built a wall around a flame.

Slowly, through many lives, we remove it brick by brick to feel its warmth and follow its light; or, we build it, wall by wall until the flame goes out, and we are convinced there is only shadow. So long have we lived in darkness.
They stopped by the roadside and Surinda tended to Frau Köehler.

When they had rejoined Rajah at his practice to leave the mules and travel again by cart, he had given her medicine because she had a fever and now, he was concerned it was getting worse. He gave her the drink he had made in the mountains and mopped her brow which was damp with sweat.

They would be back soon, and he could make her more comfortable. Rudgwick sat with her, and so that she could lay out in the back Frau Bergmeier climbed into Surinda's cart and he assured her they would be back in Bombay within the hour.

'Have you decided what you will do with your mine Frau Bergmeier?' he asked.

'It is difficult, Doctor. I...often find it hard to make decisions about important matters. There are always so many conflicting thoughts, with so many different outcomes.'

He nodded and chuckled, and reflected on the many crossroads where each of us must choose which path to take.

'Sometimes I cannot make up my mind what I want from life, 'said Frau Bergmeier, gazing at the passing fields and drifting clouds.

Surinda smiled kindly.

'We are full of contradictions, because, inside, we are many people. Each wishing to journey somewhere different. Like a team of oxen never pulling together. So, the destination is never reached.

Many people.

Some, we only see in our dreams.'

‘I have had many dreams here, since I arrived,’ said Frau Bergmeier.

‘Strange things can happen in the mountains,’ he said.

‘Not long after Faulkner had arrived and his team had abandoned him, I found him wandering in the hills, delirious and disoriented.

He told a strange tale full of wonder and confusion.

Finding himself amidst the rugged peaks of Maharashtra, in the heart of the Indian mountains, where mystique and ancient legends whisper through the winds, he had ascended the steep slopes when a strange energy had enveloped the air, tinged with an otherworldly aura.

That fateful evening, as the sun dipped below the horizon, casting long shadows across the mountainous terrain, Faulkner stumbled upon a hidden cave veiled in the mists of time, whilst searching for herbs to eat and sweet water to drink.

Intrigued, he cautiously entered, guided by an inexplicable force that beckoned him deeper into the cavern's depths.

Torch in hand, the flickering flames danced on the cavern walls, revealing intricate carvings that spoke of a divine presence.

In the heart of the cave, bathed in an ethereal glow, he beheld the magnificent form of the Goddess Kali.

Her multiple arms adorned with symbolic weapons, a garland of skulls draped around her neck, and her eyes ablaze with fury and compassion.

Time seemed to stand still as Faulkner, awestruck, witnessed the divine manifestation before him.

He said the Goddess spoke to him, her voice a harmonious blend of thunderous echoes and soothing whispers, recounting tales of ancient battles, cosmic cycles, and the dance of creation and destruction.

Faulkner, humbled by the encounter, listened intently as Kali unveiled her secrets, transcending the boundaries of mortal comprehension.

As the encounter unfolded, he felt an inexplicable connection to the divine, as if the threads of destiny were weaving a tapestry that intertwined his mortal existence with the cosmic forces at play.

Kali, Frau Bergmeier, in her wisdom, bestowed upon him visions of the past, glimpses of the future, and the understanding that balance and harmony were the keys to navigating the intricate dance of life.

Eventually, as dawn painted the sky with hues of gold, the divine presence began to fade. The cave returned to its silent slumber, and Faulkner, profoundly changed, emerged into the crisp mountain air.

The encounter with Kali had left an indelible mark on his soul, and he descended the slopes with newfound purpose, carrying the wisdom of the Goddess into the realms of the mortal and divine.

Kali, Frau Bergmeier, the formidable goddess, reigns supreme over the mountains of Maharashtra with an aura of both awe and terror.

Cloaked in darkness, her blue skin glistens with the shadows of the towering peaks she calls her domain. With a necklace of severed heads adorning her neck, representing the conquered demons of the mountains, she strikes madness in the hearts of those who dare to venture into her sacred abode.

Legend has it that Kali's wrath is unleashed upon those who seek to challenge the divine order or disrupt the natural balance of the mountainous landscape. Her eyes, fiery and piercing, burn with the intensity of a thousand suns, casting an ominous glow across the rocky terrain. As the wind howls through the craggy cliffs, it carries whispers of her name, striking fear into the hearts of the bravest souls.

Venturing into the mountains of Maharashtra is to enter a realm where the boundaries between the mortal and the divine blur. Kali, with her multiple arms, wields an assortment of weapons, each symbolising a facet of her power – destruction, creation, and the cyclical nature of existence. Those who witness her dance of cosmic chaos are left mesmerised, their fates intertwined with the whims of this formidable goddess.

Yet, amid the terror, there exists a profound reverence for Her. She is not merely a force of destruction but a symbol of the eternal cycle of life, death, and rebirth. Devotees seek her blessings, acknowledging that her ferocity is a necessary aspect of the cosmic order.

Pilgrims embark on treacherous journeys to the peaks, where they offer prayers to appease her and seek her guidance in navigating the tumultuous journey of existence.

In the shadows of the Maharashtra Mountains, her presence remains an enduring testament to the complexity of divinity. A goddess both feared and revered, embodying the inexorable forces that shape the tapestry of existence in the lofty realms where mortals tread cautiously, mindful of the goddess who strikes madness into the blood of those who dare to challenge the sacred sanctity of her abode.

Goddess of darkness, destruction, and death, Kali, is a symbol of Mother Nature.

From that day forward Faulkner was changed and worked in the mine with a frenzy that was alarming. Until he appeared in the storm, that night I told you of. '

They fell silent as they slowly trundled down the path. The afternoon sun slowly falling to the hills.

Frau Bergmeier turned back to look at Rudgwick and smiled gently.

Rajah was talking and laughing, and she wondered what his secret was, that he always seemed so happy, but the tale that Rajah was telling Rudgwick was far from a happy one.

'In the rugged mountains of Maharashtra, Mr Rudgwick,' said Rajah, 'amidst the solitude, the cave became an unlikely sanctuary for a group of women who had weathered life's storms as prostitutes. Seeking refuge from a society that had cast them aside, they found an unexpected protector in this grotesquely deformed British officer, a recluse hiding from a world that he believed had shunned him but was more a victim of his own pride and arrogance.

Scarred both physically and emotionally, he discovered solace in the company of the marginalized women of the village who

had been brought to Bombay under false pretences by ruthless people offering them a better life.'

Rajah explained that, despite societal prejudices, the colonel had extended a hand of kindness, shielding them from the cruelty of sailors and villagers who sought to perpetuate their suffering.

In the shadowy depths of the cave, a fragile alliance was forged between outcasts, a bond built on mutual survival and understanding.

Faulkner's distorted appearance mirrored the society's twisted perceptions, yet his heart bore an empathy that transcended physical deformities.

As the prostitutes had brought him sustenance pilfered from the local villages - food, fruit, and stolen wine - he became their silent guardian, a beacon of compassion in a world that he had turned his back on.

In this unlikely refuge, a microcosm of shared humanity emerged, the women, once scorned and abused, found a haven where their stories were acknowledged, where his protection became a shield against the harsh judgments of the outside world. The stolen goods served as offerings, tokens of gratitude for the sanctuary and protection he provided and the compassion he showed.

Amidst the rugged landscape and the secrets held within the cave, a fragile community had formed, challenging the norms of a society steeped in judgment.

'In the heart of Maharashtra's mountains Mr Rudgwick, this grotesque officer and the marginalized women etched an unconventional tale of resilience, kindness, and the unlikely bonds that can blossom in the most unexpected corners of the world.

A lone and deformed British officer had sought refuge in the cradle of solitude; a desolate cave hidden away from the prying eyes of a judgmental world. The officer, whose name echoed in the whispers of the wind as The Black and White God, bore both the scars of war and the weight of his own pride.

The cave, a natural sanctuary draped in shadows and silence, became a haven for him to escape the piercing gazes and murmurs that haunted him.

As he retreated into the cold embrace of the mountainous sanctuary, the once rigid contours of his face softened, releasing the tension etched by years of conformity. Alone in the company of silence, the echoes of societal expectations faded into the background. Stripped of the uniform that signified duty and decorum, he found solace in the simplicity of solitude. His deformed features, once a source of shame and ostracization, now found acceptance within the cave's silent walls and the kindness of these woman of misfortune. But he never took advantage of their vulnerability; anything they gave was given willingly.

Yet, burdened as he was, he grappled with the internal storm that raged within. Pride, like an unwelcome companion, clung to him even in isolation. The cave, though a refuge from external judgment, became the stage for an internal reckoning.

Days turned into weeks, and weeks into months, as his solitary existence in the mountains shaped his psyche.

The jagged edges of his character gradually eroded, revealing vulnerabilities he had long suppressed. The cave, in its silent wisdom, bore witness to the transformation of a man haunted by the external scars of war and the internal scars of arrogance.

You see, Mr Rudgwick, in seclusion we confront the essence of our being. The mountains of Maharashtra stand as silent witnesses to the tale of a deformed British officer who sought refuge in isolation, finding not only respite from the judgmental world but also a profound metamorphosis of his own soul where his wounds became wisdom, and his suffering healed the scars of his heart.

Perhaps, Mr Rudgwick, we must all ask ourselves, how deep are we prepared to venture into the cave?

What secrets would the shadows reveal in the depths of our own darkness.'

24. BOMBAY.

Torrential rain and lightning made Bombay a dangerous place as they arrived in the late afternoon. Hotel staff were sweeping the reception which had flooded, always concerned that snakes could be lurking in the water.

Frau Köehler was carried up to her hotel room by the staff and laid carefully in her bed. She was delirious and hallucinating. Rudgwick and Frau Bergmeier were deeply distressed as they closed the shutters.

'Without any disrespect, Doctor, would you mind if we contacted Mr Chandler, the ships surgeon, so we can get a wider perspective of her illness?'

'Of course,' said Surinda kindly, 'It is always good to get a second opinion. I must regretfully return to my practice as I have responsibilities there.'

'Thank you, Doctor,' said Rudgwick.

'Perhaps you could eventually contact me when you have decided what you wish to do with your mine, Frau Bergmeier, and I shall finalise the documents with Mr Rudgwick's help.'

Surinda spoke to the waiting staff standing anxiously by the door and told them not to leave her unattended. He gave Frau Köehler another sip of his mountain drink and she fell into a deep sleep.

'She will rest now,' said Surinda.

'You should both refresh yourselves and get some rest. She will be safe here.'

Rudgwick looked at the staff, who seemed quite young. One was missing an eye and the other appeared to stoop.

'You must call us if she wakes,' insisted Rudgwick. They both nodded.

When the room was empty, they both walked over to Frau Köehler, who was now sleeping peacefully, and felt her forehead and neck. They looked at each other and smiled.

25. CHANDLER ARRIVES.

As Mr Chandler climbed the stairs and walked along the corridor, he saw two members of staff scurry down the servant's stairs. One turned and looked back nervously. He appeared to have lost an eye.

As he entered Frau Köehler's room, after knocking, he found her sitting up in bed. 'Why Mr Chandler, how kind of you to visit.'

'You appear to have improved,' said Chandler suspiciously.

'I have indeed. In fact, I feel quite elated.'

Her smiling face was radiant as Frau Bergmeier and Rudgwick entered the room.

'Frau Köehler!' they exclaimed.

'You look radiant. I am so relieved.'

'What were you given?' said Chandler, noticing that she had pushed something under her pillow as she adjusted it.

'I... just woke from a deep sleep and after talking with the staff, who were very kind, I felt quite euphoric.'

He took her pulse, looked into her eyes and stepped back.

'Is she recovered Mr Chandler?' asked Rudgwick.

'Her pulse is heightened but she appears... stable, we must wait and see.'

'May I get up, doctor?'

‘Only to sit at the window for air. Keep the fans off.’

‘I’m ravenous!’ she exclaimed.

Frau Bergmeier and Rudgwick willingly left to arrange food, thanking the doctor and shaking his hand.

Alone with her, Chandler asked, ‘Did the staff give you anything, Frau Köehler?’

She seemed defensive.

‘Why...no Doctor Chandler. Only their kindness.’

He detected a faint smell of lead and sweet vanilla as he left to speak with the Hotel manager.

~

The next morning Frau Bergmeier returned after a restful night's sleep.

‘They will bring up some breakfast my dear friend,’ she said, taking her hand.

Frau Köehler pulled away angrily.

‘Why would I want breakfast! Why would I want anything!’ she shouted. ‘Just go away and leave me alone! I don't want to see you. Any of you!’

Frau Bergmeier was lost for words at the sudden change in her friend and deeply shocked, she backed away.

‘I’ll leave you to rest.’

‘Just get out! Get out!’

~

Frau Bergmeier hammered frantically on Rudgwick's door, trying, between her tears of hysteria, to tell him what had happened.

They both rushed to the reception clerk and asked where Chandler's clinic was.

They told him that Frau Köehler was not to be left alone and that she had become ill again.

The rain was falling, and thunder sounded as they rushed out into the street.

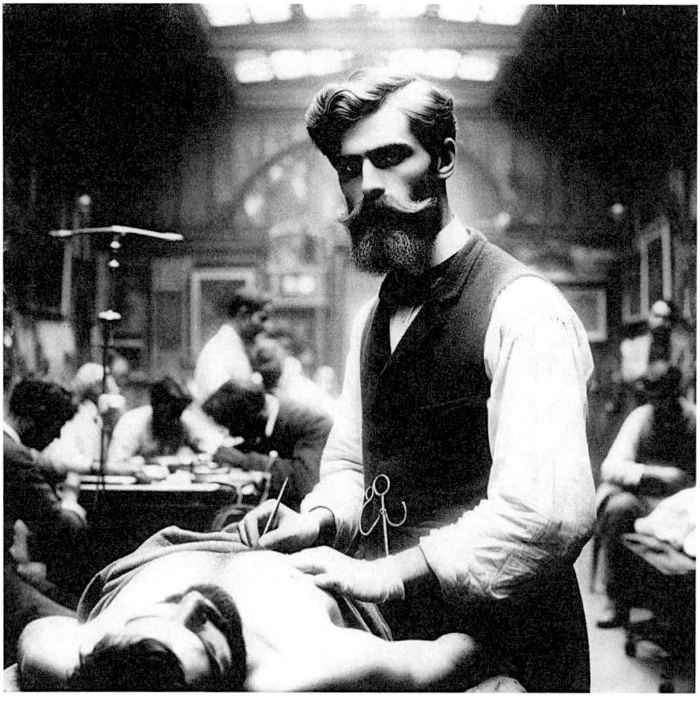

26. AT CHANDLER'S CLINIC.

They walked down a labyrinth of decaying houses, leaking sewage and rotting detritus. The clinic was in a huge, abandoned factory near the rusting pipeline, and queues of people lay huddled on the damp pavements waiting to be admitted, pleading with the orderly to be allowed to enter and see the doctors.

Babies left with young children, so as not to lose their place, had slept for days in cardboard boxes covered with newspapers.

Frau Bergmeier and Rudgwick walked past them, covering their mouths from the smell of raw sewage floating in the ditches where wandering oxen had urinated and lay dying in the stagnant water.

The orderly was shocked to see them but didn't question them as they rushed in.

The scene that greeted them struck them with horror. Bodies lay on broken slats of wooden beds and everywhere the smell of death filled their nostrils.

Chandler emerged from an area draped in woollen sheeting, his apron covered in blood. He placed a saw into a bucket filled with disinfectant and the stench of chemicals made them retch.

'Why are you here?!' shouted Chandler.

‘Frau Köehler has become erratic and aggressive, Mr Chandler’ pleaded Frau Bergmeier, near to tears. 'Are you able to come to her? I have never seen her so changed.’

Chandler sat on a stool, exhausted, and washed his hands. The blood streamed down the rivulets in the mud of the waterlogged floor.

‘You should not be here... I will come.'

Screams came from the covered room.

The Hotel manager came running into the factory, out of breath and sweating profusely.

‘She is gone, Madam! We went to care for her, but she had gone! The two waiters who were charged to attend her did not turn up for work today!’

Another surgeon came out and Chandler took him aside.

‘Her eyes were dilated. I'm sure they had given her opium,' said Chandler.

'Where would they have taken her?’ asked Rudgwick.

‘Was she white?’ asked the other surgeon.

‘Yes’

‘Then probably the opium dens of Pradarishtra Street, where they keep the European women.'

'It is dangerous, Chandler. You must notify the police,’ he whispered.

'The police here are limited,’ said Chandler. ‘Mainly concerned with social order and unrest.’

But he told the manager to take Frau Bergmeier back to the hotel and keep her safe and to contact the local constable and tell him to bring a force to Pradarishtra Street.

‘We must go ahead, Rudgwick. It is important we move quickly.’

‘If not,’ said his fellow doctor. ‘She could be sold and taken to another city.'

Chandler collected his pistol and several knives, one of which he gave to Rudgwick, who tucked it in his belt.

'The weather is bad so they may not be able to move her so soon,’ added Chandler.

They hurried out into the torrential rain and made their way down darkened lanes, winding their way to the opium dens of Pradarishtra.

For hours they entered den after den, threatening the guardians and searching amongst the prostrate intoxicated bodies strewn on the floors in stupor.

Chandler lifted one of the guards up by his neck and held a knife to his throat.

‘A new white woman! Where!?’ he shouted in his face.

Desperately trying to breath and writhing in terror, he pointed across the road. Chandler threw him aside as if he were garbage and burst into the opposite den terrifying the guards who were so drugged they were powerless to resist.

‘Where is she?!’

The guard pointed to the back room and chuckled hysterically.

They both made their way through open rooms where almost naked women lay unconscious. As they reached the end of the corridor a guard was sitting on a stool, eating. Chandler fell upon him plunging his knife into his throat and snapping his neck.

They kicked open the door.

Frau Köehler was almost unconscious on the couch. Her clothes had been ripped and she lay nearly naked but smiling. She was inhaling through a pipe heated over an oil lamp, as the liquid bubbled, and she inhaled the vapours.

Chandler knocked it out of her hand. They picked her up and Rudgwick put his coat around her, carrying her out into the rain.

The police swarmed into the dens and screams and shots were heard as they left the slums heading back to the safety of the Hotel.

Rudgwick gave Frau Köehler to the hotel staff, and they carried her carefully up to her room and placed her gently in the bed.

Frau Bergmeier and Rudgwick sat with her all night.

27. BACK AT THE HOTEL.

Chandler sat in the hotel lobby and was brought a bottle of whisky but after a few drinks he fell asleep from exhaustion.

He woke slowly in the morning and saw Rudgwick sitting opposite him. He shook himself awake.

'How is she?' he asked. Rudgwick sat staring at him.

'How is she?' he repeated. Rudgwick slowly raised his head.

'She died.'

He took an intake of breath.

'She died, Chandler!'

He burst into tears and fell forward with his head in his hands, sobbing uncontrollably. Rudgwick pulled himself together and poured himself a drink. Time had lost its meaning.

'Forgive my...unmanly outburst.'

'Masculinity does not always mean insensitivity, Rudgwick.'

He poured himself a drink even though it was early in the morning.

'It saddens me that I was not able to save her.'

'The work you do, Chandler, is beyond all human hopes or expectations.'

‘Every crisis is an opportunity, but… some just overwhelm you, and you must just accept your failure and hope you learn.’

‘Whatever you may believe, Mr Chandler, they believe you are heaven sent.’

‘Forgive my cynicism, you are a young man and full of hope, but people are naive about life. They expect too much. It's brutal. Savage. Those in power will always fill the feeble-minded with fairytales. They are willing accomplices in a global fantasy. They need it. They need to believe there is something beyond this overwhelming morass of despair. This perpetual decay. This desperation and meaninglessness.

This ocean of blood!’

They both sat in silence. The hotel was still, and the world seemed to be sleeping.

28. AT THE BEDSIDE.

Chandler and Rudgwick stood inside the door of Frau Köehler's room. Frau Bergmeier lay beside her with her dearest friend in her arms. She had lain there all night.

It was a pitiful sight, and it was some time before they could persuade her to leave the room with them.

Eventually she rose from the bed and kissing her tenderly on her forehead, she walked out with Rudgwick.

Chandler stood by the bed and pulled the sheet gently over her head. He was about to walk out when he noticed a small bottle on the balcony table.

'What is this?' he asked Rudgwick.

'It was a drink of herbs collected in the mountains and given by Doctor Surinda.' he said gently guiding Frau Bergmieir out.

Chandler smelt the drink, replaced the cork, and put it in his pocket. Pulling back the sheet he looked at Frau Köehler's tongue, tasted the moisture in her eye ducts and checked her skin. The taste of salt lingered on his lips.

He replaced the sheet, gently stroked her head and left the room.

~

The next morning, the duchess's carriage arrived at the hotel and her luggage was brought into the reception.

The hotel manager greeted her warmly, but sadly imparted the unfortunate incident that had happened. Her normally robust composure vanished in an instant and she was helped to a chair and given smelling salts.

'She was such a delicate soul. A feather floating on the wind.'

She looked across at Frau Bergmeier as Rudgwick comforted her. Two innocent souls that in the ripeness of life had spoiled like peaches.

In the short time she had known them, she had seen the indelible mark of sorrow creep into their nature like an uninvited guest.

In the dim and desolate corridors of the human soul, there exists a spectre that goes by the name of Sadness, a spectral companion that weaves its insidious tendrils around the very fabric of one's being. Most are familiar with her face. It is not a fleeting emotion, a passing storm of the heart, but rather a brooding presence that takes up residence, an unwelcome lodger in the chambers of the spirit. When part of the heart dies it leaves an empty place where grief, that lonely warrior, lays down her head, and breathes her breath of shadows in the darkened corners of the mind.

A melancholic fog that casts a perpetual shadow over the once-joyful countenance. It is as if the heart, burdened with the weight of unspoken sorrows, labours under an invisible shroud that no amount of sunlight can penetrate.

In the quiet hours of the night, when the world is hushed in slumber, sadness emerges from her hidden corners, creeping like a phantom through the labyrinths of our memory. She whispers forgotten regrets and plays the mournful melodies of yesteryears, casting a sepulchral pallor over the dreams that were once the exuberance of youth.

And so, as the days unfold, sadness becomes an integral part of one's nature, an indelible ink that stains the parchment of the soul. She is etched into the lines of a furrowed brow, reflected in the watery gaze of eyes that have witnessed the ebb and flow of life's tribulations.

As we navigate the cobblestone streets of existence with a burdened heart and footsteps heavy with the weight of sorrow, the very air one breathes seems laden with the poignant scent of what once was and can never be again.

Yet, she thought, in the melange of human experience, even sadness has its role to play. It is a sombre maestro conducting the symphony of the soul, adding depth and resonance to the otherwise frivolous notes of fleeting joy.

And so, we learn to live with this haunting companion. A companion that, though unwelcome, becomes an inseparable part of the intricate mosaic of one's existence.

‘I do not believe I shall ever recover from this Mr Rudgwick,' said Frau Bergmeier.

'I have brought her to this end.

If you could have seen how innocent and beautiful she was when we first met at the conservatoire. Barely sixteen.

She bounced into my life like a playful puppy, so trusting. So full of fun and nonsense. So full of hope. Why is it that people always die around me?'

Rudgwick sat silently gently holding her hand.

Chandler walked down the hotel staircase, lost in thought. The duchess rose to meet him.

She had had considerable time on her arduous journey from Delhi to ponder how best to help someone so obviously deserving of support.

'Mr Chandler. I feel I owe you a profound apology for misjudging you. My assumptions were decidedly incorrect, and it is a deep lesson I shall learn. I would not want you to think I am without humility.

The goodness in people is not always so obviously apparent. Please forgive me.'

He nodded and smiled.

There was an awkward silence.

'Are you able to help these unfortunate people?' she asked.

'I try. Each voyage I make, I bring what medicine I can afford and the care I can. But... I fear it is a losing battle.'

'I met with the viceroy in Delhi and pleaded for more funds for you, but I fear he does not see it as a pressing problem. As is always the case in politics, unless they smell the blood, the wheels will keep creaking until they finally succumb to rust and corrosion.'

She sat in a chair and asked him to sit with her.

'Because of the unfortunate demise of Colonel Faulkner, I am now in possession of considerable funds that I was granted to help him and the women who had been lured here from broken lives in England, and who had hoped for something better.

After the police raid, these unfortunate women are now in the city jail, when they should be in hospital.

Clearly, from what I have heard, the facilities at your temporary clinic are far from satisfactory, so would you consider helping me to build a new hospital, whose primary function would be to heal the women who have fallen foul of such despicable criminals, who's only aim is to fulfil their own desires?'

Chandler sat and stared at the duchess, somewhat lost for words.

'It would also enable you to provide better care for the ill and needy in Bombay,' she added,

'But that would entail me relinquishing my post as ship's surgeon.'

'Indeed, but you would be given, in recompense, the opportunity to run a hospital that would bear your name.'

Chandler was taken aback at such generosity.

'Clearly I would not expect you to decide now, so perhaps you could let me know your decision at your earliest convenience, but, Tempus fugit, Mr Chandler!'

She stood.

Chandler smiled, rose from his chair and warmly shook her hand.

'We have a moral obligation to a country in our care.' he said.

'Indeed we do, Mr Chandler. Indeed we do. And I'm sure, once the hospital is functioning, it will attract further funding from those who wish to be associated with such a worthy cause.'

'It would be easy for me to be cynical, duchess. Perhaps because I have seen and experienced suffering. Our societies with their unfortunate and destitute are not underpinned by the equal distribution of wealth but supported by the charities and philanthropic organisations that flourish, without which many unfortunate people would languish and die, and without which our societies would crumble.

Even so, it would be comforting to believe that these gestures come from a genuine desire to uplift the needy and fulfil what they believe is their Christian duty, but it is more likely that the motivation comes from an investment in Paradise, the desire to save our own souls, etched into consciousness through millennia of history and the fear of retribution, not from the kindness of the human heart, which always barters for its compassion.'

'You may be right. I believe humanity is disenchanted with itself, Mr Chandler. It feels as if we are permanently hovering on the threshold of disaster. Staring into the abyss of war which seems to be a convenient way to rid the governments of their undervalued youth. Why else would they send them to the fields of slaughter as sacrificial lambs on the altar of hubris.

I believe if you were to ask any mother, honestly, whether she would rather have the glory of victory, or her beloved sons and husbands back in the bosom of the family, she would choose the latter.

The laurels of death serve little purpose but to haunt us from the grave,'

Chandler shook his head as if grappling with the insanity of existence.
'Why must we fight for a nation that has never given a damn about us? Robbed us of ambition, shattered out dreams, and used us to build a fantasy of imperialism - the monster of Empire.'

She saw the futility of war and the bitterness of loss and neglect etched upon his face.

'They fight...to preserve our way of life, Mr Chandler. And, like love, we rarely learn its value until we have lost it.'

'Whose way of life are we speaking of duchess? Love and life are the legacies of bewilderment.
It is the brutal and often bitter realisation that love is always self-serving, and that compassion, loyalty, care and kindness are infinitely more rewarding. That is why in the end we seem to value our friends more than our lovers.
Love is a biological force of attraction, and if we're lucky we make the transition from romantic to cynic without the bitter pangs of regret and disillusion. We ask too much of life, too much of people.
One day we must put aside the fairy tales and bedtime stories. We are merely parasites that feed upon each other, in an eternal quest to survive in a bleak and barren mystery, without answers, without purpose.
Please, do not misunderstand me duchess, I neither accuse nor judge. We are only victims of a mystery, we cannot comprehend.'

She sensed a deep sadness in his demeanour, and suspected his darkness of spirit had other causes.

She placed a gentle hand on his arm.

'Frau Köehler had a very fragile grip on life, Mr Chandler. You did all you could to save her.'

'I have no wish to discuss it.'

He bowed and thanked the duchess, who descended into a large armchair with a lingering melancholy.

Sometimes, sadly, she thought, there cannot be a meeting of minds. But she respected the man and sensed that he was more compassionate than he admitted to, despite a numbness of the heart. But she had done her best and offered what help she could to a man and a cause she considered worthy.

She watched him walk out of the hotel pursued by a trail of adoring children, like a Pied Piper without his flute.

And lost in a momentary reverie, as one sometimes is, she found herself observing a man who to all outward appearance had seemed cold and distant, or closed to everything but his duty to humanity, an island to himself in little need of comfort or tenderness, a wound inflicted by the legacy of betrayal or the folly of trust.

In the shadowy recesses of the human heart, there exists a profound numbness; a chill that settles upon the soul like a thick fog, rendering it impervious to the warmth of joy and the tender caress of hope. It is a malady not easily diagnosed, for it festers in the hidden corners, masked by the facade of everyday existence.

The affliction is the consequence of life's relentless pummelling, a relentless barrage that leaves the heart scarred and calloused.

In the hallowed halls of healing, both of body and spirit, there lay an enigma as confounding as any mystery. The physicians of the soul, be they philosophers or therapists, seek to unravel the intricacies of disillusionment - the slow erosion of dreams, the gradual fading of once-vivid aspirations. The heart, once an open book eager to absorb the tales of life, becomes an ancient tome whose pages are weathered and torn, each chapter etched with the bitter ink of experience.

Yet, in the quest for redemption, she thought, one often encounters a closed door, its formidable presence a symbol of the barriers erected by the trials of life.

The key to unlock this door, to breach the fortress of numbness, eludes many a weary traveller. Some spend their days searching, a Sisyphean endeavour to unearth the elusive key that might liberate their embattled hearts.

Others resign themselves to a barren existence, their dreams entombed behind an impenetrable barrier.

As the spectre haunts the corridors of the heart, the world itself takes on a sombre hue. What was once vibrant and full of promise becomes a landscape shrouded in mist, where the contours of hope and happiness blur into indistinct shapes. The disillusioned soul, burdened by the weight of unmet expectations, stumbles through this obscured terrain, desperately seeking solace in a world that seems indifferent to its plight.

And so, we confront the enigma of the closed door; a metaphor for the myriad struggles that life imposes upon the human spirit. Whether this door remains forever locked or yields to the persistent efforts of the heart's intrepid seeker, only time will tell. The psychology of healing, the

disillusionment and redemption, unfolds like a narrative woven with the threads of human resilience and the relentless pursuit of an elusive key.

A key that, as yet, she also had not found. Or had she ceased her quest? And like Chandler, now languished in a life of service. A life devoid of passion or love.

And as she watched Chandler and the children disappear into a sea of colour she wondered why, in this sometimes perverse existence she had always learned more about the true nature of life from her suffering, than from her joy.

29. SURINDA'S CLINIC.

Surinda sorted through his mail before he began his practice. Patients had already begun to assemble outside since dawn, while it was still cool.

He opened an official letter from the Cellular jail, on the island of Kālā Pānī. It informed him that there had been an attempted escape of two hundred and thirty inmates from the prison. Most had been captured trying to leave the island, some had been put into solitary confinement, and eighty-seven had been hanged. A handful had managed to escape pretending to be fishermen.

One prisoner, Bhagat Kishore, had come from Surinda's district and he was to keep a watch and notify the authorities if he turned up. He was dangerous and should not be approached.

Surinda placed the letter back in the envelope, finished his tea, and opened his surgery.

~

It had been a long day for him, and the fan had given him a headache, so he closed early. Locking the door and the shutters, so it was cooler in the shade, he walked to a back room and opened the door.

'Come out Bhagat,' he whispered.

Bhagat stuffed the food Surinda had put on the table and gulped down some Desi Daru from a jug.

'The Elders from the village were put in the jail because they had given themselves up, even though it was mainly for us political prisoners,' said Bhagat.'Many guards were killed. It was mayhem. They hanged many. Tortured others. Inquilab Zindabad! Inquilab Zindabad!'

'Be quiet, you fool!' whispered Surinda.

He went to the window and peered through the shutters, but all was calm.

'Keep me safe and I will make you rich,' said Bhagat.

'What do you mean?'

'Before the Elders from your village starved to death, while they were delirious, they told me how they had hidden the veins of gold in the cave. Yes. I know about it! They laughed and said that no one would ever find it. Take me there and I will show you!'

Surinda was worried, but this could help many people, he thought.

'I will need protection, food and provisions and I will work for you. It will be good for us both! Surinda was less concerned for his own gain but thought it would be good to continue the Colonel's legacy if it were true.'

'Sleep tonight,' he said, locking the door. 'We will leave in the morning at dawn.'

30. THE DUCHESS VISITS THE JAIL.

Despite the hotel manager's protestations, the duchess was determined to visit the jail. She also demanded that several staff accompany her. Rudgwick and Frau Bergmeier were determined to also go. She had been shrewd enough to bring a photographer along with her to hold their actions to account.

At the local holding facility, she marched past the terrified soldiers and burst into the commissioner's office who was having his dinner. He stumbled out of his chair in astonishment, frantically buttoning his tunic and choking on his food.

'I am the Duchess of Beaufort here at the request of the viceroy in Delhi and I demand you release the seven European women into my care! They should be in a hospital, sir, not in a prison!'

Her voice was so loud that people in the street outside congregated and peered through the window.

'I really must...'

'Now sir! Now!'

'Yes. Yes of course... I was only... er. We were only keep...'

She glared at him, and he led her to the cells, giving her a very wide berth.

She was a formidable presence and in full sail would intimidate anyone that defied her will.

The hotel manager arrived with Chandler.

The jail cell was crowded with women. Some sleeping, some crying, some confused or angry. This was not moral reform but incarceration and long-term isolation.

The cell was filthy and smelt of urine and menstrual blood - rat infested.

There were Indian women, white women, prostitutes, drug addicts, transvestites, anyone the Empire considered criminal or sexually deviant, silencing a society that before had been tolerant of fluidity. They were now thrown together like so much human waste.

An old Muslim woman sidled up to an English white girl crouching by the bars.

'My father was a sepoy for the East India tea company. He refused to suck on a bullet with pig's lard for the British rifles, so they shot him. Others they incarcerated for life, fettered, forever hidden from the sun. I have been in and out of prison all my life. I hate the British.'

A transvestite called "The Lizard" squirmed across the cell, nudging the unconscious woman, sniffing and licking the floor. He slithered up the wall to a woman sitting in the corner of the cell.

'They bound my hands and pulled my arms over my head, dislocating my shoulders. And...hot pokers? I won't tell you what they did with those!'

He spat and showed his teeth.

'I am still pretty. No?'

He smiled coquettishly and edged closer, his eyes bulging from his sockets.

'Do you know in the mountains there are women who never cut the placenta? Once you cut, you breathe, you eat, you are dependent on the world.'

He looked around nervously.

'They soak the sack in herbal mixtures that preserve it.'

He started to laugh loudly, hysterically. The guards rushed in and beat him mercilessly with bamboo sticks until he pleaded for them to stop. They threw a blanket over him and dragged him out by his feet.

'No please! Please!'

The guard turned to the women who were barely conscious. They looked up with glazed eyes.

'He is mad. Crazy mad.'

The guard slammed the cell door and threw the chain around the bars, securing the lock. Some women were already withdrawing, hallucinating, and screaming.

31. AT THE HOTEL.

The women were carried to the hotel and the duchess instructed the manager to give them her suite and she would move into a smaller room. She assured them that all expenses or damage would be covered.

'How long will it be before they will be normal Mr Chandler?' asked the manager.

'It depends how long they have been addicted. A week. A month. Maybe longer.'

Chandler instructed him that he would need a regular supply of clean water for washing but also for dehydration.

'I have medicine and will gradually reduce the dose. It will help, but it will not be pleasant.'

'What can we expect?' said the duchess.

'Aggression, vomiting, diarrhoea, sweating. They will need things to distract them. Books, magazines. Music.

'I will play for them,' said Frau Bergmeier. 'It will heal me too.'

'Poor darlings. They look so young,' said the duchess.

Chandler examined each of the women.

'I will have a clearer picture once one of them is fully conscious and I can talk with her. I will have to return to the clinic, but they need to be watched constantly. Lock the windows and doors.'

'I will stay and care for them as best I can,' said Rudgwick.

He noticed that Frau Burgmeier's usually decisive nature had undergone a dramatic change. The grief at the loss of her dearest friend had left an emptiness within her, and he was concerned that she had lost her way.

One of the young women appeared to be waking up and started vomiting and sweating profusely. Chandler administered what help he could. But for those trapped in the terrible spiral of addiction little could be done other than witness the pitiable effects of withdrawal.
After a while she became calmer but had lost control of her movements and suffered the embarrassment of diarrhoea. The duchess stepped forward.

'Gentlemen, leave this to me,' she said. 'Please give her privacy, so she can maintain at least a semblance of dignity.'

Chandler reluctantly left for his clinic and Rudgwick closed the door, leaving Frau Bergmeier to assist.

She seemed grateful to have some purpose, grateful to lay aside for a while the aching pain that was robbing her of her sanity.

~

The weeks passed and the city was lashed with violent rain and winds. Ships were confined to harbour and those at anchor were brought within the harbour walls and lashed together for safety to prevent them from capsizing. Some were lifted in the raging storm and thrown across the shore, snapping like old bones, brittle and frangible.

The city slums were flooded, and people saved what they could and brought them to shelter. Many starved. No supply ships could arrive, and some sank at sea, lost in an unforgiving ocean.

The dens in Pradasrashtra Street collapsed as walls crumbled and people were carried off in the storm. Bodies were washed away in the raging torrent descending from the mountains and swept out into the ocean, whose waves, like water monsters, mercilessly lashed the city. As if Amphitrite in her anger laughed as the Nereids danced and made merry in the waves.

Fragile wood shelters were cast in their hundreds to the wind and flew across the city like prehistoric birds.

Hotels rushed to put sandbags at their entrances. Carpets were lifted and furniture placed on bricks to prevent them from disintegrating in the rising water flow.

Many died from the snakes in the mountain streams that flowed down into the city and carried death in their wake.

Cemeteries were washed with flowing mudslides, and cadavers floated passed the houses and hotels on higher ground as people watched with horror a floating procession of decomposing corpses. A Mardi Gras and carnival of death.

~

The whole top floor of the hotel was now in effect a hospital. Provisions from the hotel larder had helped them survive the weeks of isolation as the storm raged.

The women slowly recovered, their strength grew, and their complexion improved.

From endless hours of talking and reading aloud they had regained the spirit that had been so mercilessly beaten from them. And each of them became an ardent admirer of Mr Chandler, who had visited daily, and despite their aggression had treated them with a tenderness and humour that impressed everyone.

One, he could not save, and she died on the first night.

The duchess sat next to Frau Bergmeier. Together they listened to the rain tapping at the window. The storm had passed, and the final drops were falling from the trees, resplendent palms that towered above them and had proudly survived the onslaught.

'The worst has passed it seems,' said the duchess, gently touching Frau Bergmeier's shoulder.

'Has it?'

She looked at her the way a mother might, tenderly, and knowing it was a journey that only she could make, and all she could do was walk beside her.

'I wish I had never brought her here, duchess.'

'India is seductive, and nothing is new,' she said. 'No pure soul claws its way into this world.

We are like a painting that has been overworked, reimagined, we lose the original, the reason, the purpose. Hidden memories we desperately claw at to find out who we are. Who we were. What we have lost. What is real and what is not. We are merely fractured pieces of ourselves we do not comprehend, reassembled, becoming a montage of contradictions. A deceitful mirror where we choose the eyes that smile or condemn and remain at their mercy.

People are very vulnerable at times of transition in their lives my dear,' she said gently. 'Death or loss. And unscrupulous people can seriously damage a sensitive soul. Rewrite their mental landscape.

In painting I believe it's called pentimenti. When the artist changes his mind and paints over the original image.

Not unlike the cunning restructuring of a person's mindset by deceitful predators promising them salvation, freedom from trauma. Offering them a naive explanation of why they are in despair by way of eclectic teachings, parables and simple myths. Creating a false eureka moment for the desolate, searching for meaning, the lost and the lonely. But ultimately, they are relinquishing control.

Because they are desperate for someone to tell them what to do. How to live. What to think. It seems to be the curse of the human race; we still need our fairy tales and bed-time stories, floundering as we are in our bewilderment.'

She put her arms around Frau Bergmeier.

'When my husband died,' said the duchess. 'I was full of guilt. His memory was a door too painful to open. But, when someone we cared about deeply is no longer there, all we have left is their spirit. In all its glory. By shutting them out, we deny everything they ever gave us. When all they want, I'm sure, is to become part of us and make us stronger. To live again within us. They give us their eyes to see the world as they did. The memory of them, is their parting gift.'

Frau Bergmeier sat in silence looking through the window. No sooner had the rain touched the glass, like tears, it dissolved.

'But we can no longer hold them.'

The duchess took her face in her hands.

'We hold them in our dreams my dear.'

Frau Bergmeier rested her head on her lap sobbing uncontrollably, and as she stroked her head the duchess whispered,

'Let it all out my dear.'

32. BOMBAY.

The rains had ceased, and a massive clean-up operation began. A system they knew well, but this time the extent of devastation was inconceivable.

Surprisingly there had only been a small outbreak of cholera on the urban plateau and the imperial government was swift to identify and isolate the people. The efficiency of the local councils was in stark contrast to the usual chaos that attended most endeavours. The control of tropical diseases was something that even the hardened dissidents agreed was maybe, in their eyes, the only positive thing brought to India by the British Empire.

'But then the passionate are always myopic,' said the duchess selecting a suitably sturdy chair on the hotel terrace.

In the mountains the remaining flood water was burnt away by the scorching heat, sucked up into billowing clouds that lour'd over the city, before passing on to unsuspecting climes.

The women were moved onto the terrace, drinking lemonade and sitting under white Punkhas.

Those who were still feeling delicate, stayed in a shady room, behind jalousies that gently filtered the light. The duchess would eventually provide them with more modest attire but for the moment she felt it was more important that they kept the rehabilitation to a minimum.

~

The Punkah Wallah had fallen asleep in the heat, he was gently prodded and woke with a start.

'Sorry Memsahib!' he shrieked and pulled the string with his toe a little too frantically.

The hotel manager walked along the terrace checking that all was in order. He moved a single chair that was slightly out of alignment. Standing back, he seemed satisfied with his work, and walked off to whatever important and detailed minutiae might demand his exceptional experience.

Lazy days turned to weeks and the city slowly began to heal.

Ships that had cracked and ruptured in the harbour were lifted, broken up, and towed away by teams of horses. The smell of damp wood and sea salt permeated the air.

Vultures swooped and pecked at floating corpses yet to be recovered.

But in amongst this pall of dazed bewildered feelings there seemed as if a new hope, a new beginning had arrived like a welcome stranger.

And the emptiness of loss crept away like a frightened ghost, knowing it had joined the bloodless and unbodied, now laying in the Tower of silence.

It had been many weeks since Surinda had visited Rajah, his closest friend, and he had much to tell.

The mountain paths had been water-logged, and the wheels of his cart stuck in the mud and made the way impassable, so he had often had to turn back.

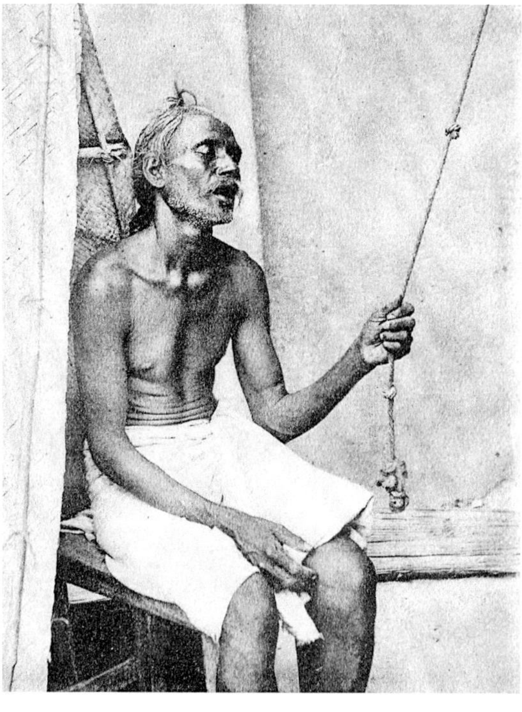

But now the earth was tinder-dry and cracked like an old man's skin.

Bhagat was left at his house until his return with instructions to keep out of sight, not to open the door to anyone, and not to drink too much.

He was excited to meet again with Frau Bergmeier and tell her what he had found in the cave.

Once the paths were cleared, he received a letter from her informing him that she would be abandoning the mine and returning to Berlin and asking him to come to Bombay as soon as he was able, when travel was possible.

The statue of Colonel Faulkner in the village had withstood the recent storm, giving comfort to the villagers whose houses had been swept away in the torrent.

It glowed and shone like new as if it knew that soon all would be well.

33. SURINDA RETURNS.

Surinda brought his oxcart to a halt, paused, and listened to the deafening sounds of birdsong. The fragrance of flora and fauna was strong in his nostrils, and wildlife was abundant, tigers often crossing his path and staring at him, as if to say...

'Are you still here old man? Oh, there are stories I could tell.'

As he ambled off into the jungle to enjoy the fruits of the earth, provided in abundance by Brahma and now renewed by Vishnu.

'Shiva will have to find another place to wreak havoc,' he chuckled and sang as the cart moved onwards down the path towards Bombay.

The storm, the influenza and cholera had raged relentlessly for weeks, bringing devastation to the population, industries and smaller enterprises, who had received little or no help from the imperial government. It swept through the city like a biblical plague.

Schools, theatres and music halls were damaged beyond recognition and many a famous face who had once made the people laugh or lifted them with celestial voices from their daily troubles were now seen working in the meat markets or toiling in the fields.

No shame in that, they were received with honour that they had embraced a new reality.

Little did they know that an old village doctor on a peasant's cart was bringing tidings that would heal and renew the city.

Many were reluctant to pander to superstitious nonsense, but even they could not deny the mysterious events that had brought such riches from a mountain cave.

34. AT THE HOTEL.

Doctor Surinda's eyes shone as he retold the story of how the cave had once again given up its treasures. They sat spellbound and were full of many questions.

'I do not understand,' said Frau Bergmeier. 'I inspected the walls carefully and found nothing but rock and coal.'

'That was because it was not in the walls, but in the floor,' explained Surinda.

'Under layers of earth there were several slabs of stone which, once removed, led to a tunnel that had been excavated by the Colonel. The veins of gold stretched many yards along the passageway and after a while it led through to another large cave, undisturbed for thousands of years.

A Cathedral, a temple of stalactites and stalagmites bursting from the hot spring. Fissures in the rock shed light onto a subterranean lake that shone in the filtered light like diamonds dancing in the sun. And scattered around the edge were many precious stones protruding from the earth or glistening in the walls. Emeralds, Rubies, Sapphires and Diamonds and many precious metals and minerals.

A veritable Aladdin's cave of wonder that even Scheherazade could not conceive. And on the walls, painted scenes of strange creatures toiling the land and tending the beasts and ascending in chairs of fire.

Strange. Curious and strange.'

He turned to Frau Bergmeier.

'So, do you still wish to close the mine madam? It belongs to you.'

35. THE FOLLOWING YEAR.

Time passed and the city experienced a new renaissance, flourishing with new hope and good fortune.

Bhagat proved a worthy manager and Rajah, overcoming his superstitions, worked the mine well for which they were both handsomely remunerated for their labour.

Wealth flowed down into the city coffers and many new projects blossomed. The theatres and music halls were rebuilt, and people laughed again, and voices were lifted that had been silenced for so long. The new Köehler academy of music, built for her dearest friend, was opened on a fine spring morning, and Frau Bergmeier played Frau Köehler's violin at the ceremony, her tears falling upon the fine and polished wood; the first time she had played in a very long while. Stained with her tears, she placed it in its case like a child's coffin.

Rudgwick had kept Malbraid, his senior partner, informed about events but he hadn't received communication from him for some time.

One day in early spring he received a letter from London informing him that Sir Ranulph Malbraid had sadly died, and that the practice had now passed into his capable hands.

Rudgwick, though of tender years, had not anticipated the depth of emotion within him.

His benefactor, a paternal figure whose benevolence extended beyond the realms of jurisprudence, had been more than a tutor, he had been a guardian spirit, a guiding luminary in the labyrinth of legal intricacies and his foolish struggles of youth.

He found himself grappling with the unexpected weight of grief. It was as though a familial tie, unbeknownst to him, had woven itself in the intricate tapestry of his heart, and now, with the cruel shears of mortality, fate had severed it abruptly.

The young lawyer grappled with the poignant truth that he had lost not only a respected friend but a surrogate father.

Sir Ranulph Malbraid stood as a testament to the enduring impact of a mentor's kindness and the indomitable spirit that outlives the confines of mortal temporality.

Rudgwick was deeply conflicted.

Having found a new meaning for his life in India, he was reluctant to leave. But he also felt a duty to continue the legacy of so fine a man.

As if by premonition Sir Ranulph had written to him, advising him that his struggles would soon be over.

'My Dearest Rudgwick,

As the shadows of mortality loom over me, I beseech you not to carry the weight of legacy, guilt, or regret upon your shoulders. Let not the chains of the past bind your spirit but embrace the unknown future that unfurls before you.

We were but ships that passed in the night, our destinies intertwining briefly on this vast sea of existence.

As I embark on my final voyage, I implore you to set sail towards the horizons of opportunity without the heavy anchors of yesteryears.

Few men have not stumbled on the thorny paths of life. And the human heart is no man's keeper. Your mother and I were a comfort to each other in her time of grief. Please forgive my silent shame at the gift that we were given. And the pride that I have felt to watch you grow into the finest of men, my dear son.

Life is a transient dance, and in the grand ballroom of time, our steps are but fleeting. Treasure the moments we shared, but do not let them shackle your journey. Have an eye to the destitute and downtrodden, the fallen and the meek.

Indeed. We must learn to give freely, but not to wastrels. Neither seeking to profit or gain. but content that the knowledge we were given we are able to pass on to another.

Few will acknowledge your help as it would be a tacit admission that they needed it. And some unfortunate people's self-esteem is as fragile as a drunkard's pledge. But we draw succour in the knowledge that generosity like charity is its own reward.

For no truer saying was ever penned than that those blest with wisdom and wealth are merely transient custodians of the gifts from God.

May you find solace, Edward, unburdened by the shadows of what might have been. That said, my dear boy, I leave you with the gift of a boundless future.

With eternal fondness, Your father, Ranulph.'

~

Frau Bergmeier had become an efficient administrator of the mine and bathed in the affection of Mr Rudgwick, both becoming ever closer.

Many of the women who had been saved by Mr Chandler had fled England from marital abuse, persecution or a broken heart. Most possessed a high degree of intelligence, and some returned to England with the duchess. All but two. One was trained by Rudgwick to manage the books and contracts from the proceeds of the mine. The other possessed some medical training and was welcomed into the new Faulkner Free Clinic to assist Mr Chandler.

Doctor Surinda declined any offers of help.

'I am a simple soul, living a simple life and my dearest wish is that I should not return and make all the same stupid mistakes again. And as someone much wiser than I once said,

'If you want to know what God thinks of money, just look at who he gives it to.'

Frau Bergmeier looked askance at him with a smile.

'But,' added Surinda, 'he does seem to have got it right this time. We must all learn from our mistakes. Even God.'

He chuckled.

Rudgwick wrote to Faulkner's widow telling her the events of her husband's life and his wish to remain anonymous because of his horrific injuries. She was deeply saddened that he had not allowed her to care for him, but she had loved and understood the man, and though not content, her heart could rest.

Rudgwick was sensitive enough to omit any gruesome details that might cause undue distress. For indeed, truth to tell, what benefits would derive for a delicate soul, to be burdened by the darker shadows of man's journey to himself.

For our deeds are known, and our agony sufficient to the day thereof.

~

Frau Bergmeier insisted that funds from the cave should still be sent to the family.

After many months of anguish, she was persuaded to sort through Frau Köehler's belongings, tenderly folding every dress, remembering each occasion she had worn them. So many memories, as she had watched her shine, heard the echoes of her laughter and shared the secret confidences of a shy creature as she hovered on the threshold of love, and, unrequited, had wiped away her tears and held her in her arms to comfort her from the brittle blades of rejection.

One evening she came upon her diary, tucked in her purse amongst the nonsense things that women treasure, remembrances to bring a smile or heal the tender bruises nursed in quiet mourning. Deep within these sheets of confession were the private dreams engraved upon her heart.

Deeply pining for her dearest friend, she opened the book in the quiet sanctity of her room and wept to read the secret longings and hopes for a life that had not yet fully blossomed.

How often, she thought, do we think we know those dearest to us. We accept their facade like a mask to shield them from the world. Make judgments, condemn or fall in love with who we think they are.

But here, within the pages of her journal were the tender moments of her heart. Her fears, her aspirations. Her quiet time in the sanctity of silence.

"December. 1880.

What is death? Are we, at birth, already held by the sticky fingers of gravity, until too weak to resist we finally succumb and plummet to an earthly bed.

And in that final fall we break the membrane of this our earthly threshold, dissolving in a bed of dust to lie with beggars and saints now food for worms. How grim, how abhorrent it seems to the waking mind, hidden in this crown of bone, this small pathetic vessel that thinks itself a builder of Gods and Kings and fragile Empires.

And in our earthly grave, are we an audience to an ever-changing scene, a witness to the ravages of time, at the mercy of the wind?

In that final shedding that strips away the husk of deceit do we become the sum of all, the prodigal dust returning once again to the fire of dreams and the embers of hope?'

Frau Bergmeier read into the long night, laughing and weeping.

And it seemed to her that in the shadows of that quiet room, while the crickets sang and the north-east monsoon had left

its anger in the Bay Of Bengal and softened to a gentle breeze that blew the Palm trees against her window, it seemed as if her friend had returned, and once more, as she so often had, caressed her cheek and shared the warmth of closeness and the whispers of innocence, the loss of which had left an emptiness in her soul.

~

The next morning as she descended the stairs, she saw Rudgwick sitting alone at the breakfast table. And for a while she stood watching him, a fleeting moment when she was overwhelmed that so much lay ahead for them. So much to share.

She looked out of the large window at the bustle of carriages in the street, the harbour beyond, a thousand people with their purposes, the restless ecstasy of life.

I love India, she thought. Rudgwick looked up and smiled.

'Another day, Mr Rudgwick. Aren't we lucky.'

He took her hand and kissed it.

'I have passed the strangest of nights Mr Rudgwick. Full of tears and laughter and sweet remembrances that warmed my heart. I imagined as I read the words of my dearest friend set down with such honesty and innocence that she stood at my shoulder, smiling, that I should share the secrets of her deepest desires, her hopes and fears, that we are never privileged to witness in the hot flush of youth, or deeper nightmares that keep us hushed and watchful as our lives pass before us ebbing away like the sand in an hourglass, reluctant to release our wildest child, fearful of our foolish mischiefs, in free fall and ecstasy abandoned and as free as the wind.

Why is it, do you suppose that I know her so much better in death than I ever did in life dear Edward?

Is death the end of secrets, are we left with only ghosts and memories, confidantes to listen to our silent longings. Without censure, without demands. Without judgement?

It is as if her voice is now buried in my heart.'

~

One of Faulkner's sons entered the military and the other had recently graduated as a physician. He received a reply to his letter to Mr Chandler granting his request to work and train at the hospital that bore his father's name.

A new statue of Ganesha, the God of new beginnings was erected, and standing below him was the handsome figure of Colonel Sir Henry Faulkner, as once he was, benefactor and hero of a new age of hope.

Written on the plaque was an inscription they had discovered much later, on the walls of the cave.

"I arrived with no fanfare. I left with no ovation.

But while I was here...

I saw,

Your love. Your hatred. Your pain. Your fear. Your tears.

Your laughter. Your confusion. Your anger. Your stupidity.

Your wisdom and compassion. Your indignation and defiance.

Your uniqueness.

I was all of these.

And it left me breathless...

to have merely been a part of it."

Eventually a new school was built, and the teachers told the enraptured children sitting at their feet...

THE STRANGE TALE

OF THE BLACK AND WHITE GOD.

EPILOGUE

A young, shy, Indian boy from Porbandar stood at the foot of the statue.

'You see Mama. There is goodness in the world.'

She stroked his head.

'Yes. There is Mohandas.'

The End

Young Gandhi

JEFF SHANKLEY

Jeff is a character actor, author and composer.

Trained at RADA (Royal Academy of Dramatic Art), he emerged as a silver medallist and went on to star in more than thirteen West-End productions.

He was a member of the Royal Shakespeare Company. He was the original Munkustrap in CATS and the original Greaseball in STARLIGHT EXPRESS; both composed by Andrew Lloyd-Webber and directed by Trevor Nunn.

He began writing during the lockdown of the Pandemic and two years later had written sixteen novels, two musicals and two libretti for opera.

THOSE WHO HAVE EYES is his debut novel to be published shortly, and THE STRANGE TALE OF THE BLACK AND WHITE GOD is his second novel.

In recent reviews the quality of Shankley's writing has been compared to Dickens, Scott-Fitzgerald, Gabriel García Márquez and Herman Melville.

Jeff lives in Suffolk UK; Puglia, Italy; and Colombo, Sri Lanka.

Arantha Photography Colombo Sri Lanka

The front cover, some images and content researched with AI.